DRAGONS YET TO SLAY

by
Vincent Lockhart

All characters in this novel are fictional, and no person, living or dead, is depicted therein.

© Copyright 1992 by Vincent Lockhart

Published by A-L Publishers
P.O. Box 370407
El Paso, TX 79937-0407

A-L Publishers
P.O. Box 370407
El Paso, TX 79937-0407

ISBN-0-9635610-0-6

Printed in the United States of America

Dragons Yet To Slay

CHAPTER ONE

Harvey Zimmerman was breathing in short, measured gasps. He sat in cell four with his bleeding hand on his knee. Blood oozed from a finger of his right hand where a fingernail should have been. The thumb was swollen and blue. His pallid face told of acute physical suffering. His body ached from the blows it had taken. Muscles were sore from the violent contractions when electric shock had been applied. His head was erect. His eyes, despite dark circles of blue, seemed to glow with defiance of his captors.

Cell four was in the basement of a great gray stone building on the south side of the mountain city of Dalat in Vietnam.

Harvey was an American.

The basement of the Bastille, as Harvey had called this three story building in years past, was the color of one of the native gray lizards, geckos. The Bastille was chilly not only in temperature but in its atmosphere of despair.

The Bastille had been built by the French of

locally quarried gray stone in the early part of the century to house French soldiers. Called *casernes* by the French, these barracks were more elaborate and permanent than the wooden, one story barracks Americans built during wars, even in the United States. The French often had used the Bastille also for offices for the mayor, sometimes district officers and other leaders as well as for the *gendarmerie*, their police. Six prison cells had been built across the northern wall of this basement. The remainder of the basement floor was open. A stairway reached up to the first floor and out to the street.

Harvey wore a dirty, torn, civilian shirt, unbuttoned, exposing red and blue blotches on his flesh, the results of shocks from an electric cattle prod. The left side of his face was purple from the blows administered by his Vietnamese police interrogators. His khaki pants were worn. His sturdy, L.L. Bean walking shoes were scraped and showed evidence of much walking before he had been captured.

Harvey had a prominent, square chin and ample black hair streaked with gray.

He had just been through another interrogation by the Vietnamese. To his own surprise, he was still alive. The Vietnamese police who had conducted the interrogation had watched with satisfaction somewhat dimmed because even violent torture had not elicited any meaningful information.

Guards had secured his thumb to the table with a carpenter's clamp. The torture team had then used a pair of pliers to rip off one of his fingernails while others asked questions.

"Why are you in Vietnam? Why were you in Dak Gle? What task has the CIA assigned to you?"

Harvey recalled the events leading to his arrest, fingerprinting and photos by the police. After about three days, the police chief had entered his cell.

"Harvey Zimmerman, American spy."

Harvey then knew the Vietnamese had sent his photo and fingerprints to the Russians for identification.

Unwilling to provide the vital intelligence information his interrogators wanted and knowing silence intensified the anger of the torture team, Harvey framed nonsensical replies that had no relation to the questions asked.

"The sky is so beautiful. The crisp mountain air gives vigor to the mind. The stars shine brightly at night."

The principal interrogator, largest of the three questioners, smashed his fist into Harvey's face, cursing him. Then the two assistants spread his legs and the interrogation team leader shoved the electric prod into Harvey's genitals. To keep from shrieking as the electricity jolted through his body, Harvey trained his mind on a scene of white beaches and faraway mountains rather than think of his briefing in Bangkok and his mission to Dak Gle.

The prisoner had been returned to his cell in the

basement.   As he sat with his throbbing hand upon his knee, he recalled that he had recognized this building as the Bastille.   During the late sixties, Harvey had been a visitor in Dalat, but now he was here as a prisoner. Was it only two weeks ago that he was brought here? It seemed like months.

He looked around his cell.   The back wall, made of eighteen inch square limestone blocks, was the original foundation of the old building.   The partition between his cell and the other cells was made of cement blocks much more modern than the quarried stone that made up the foundation and walls of this fortress.

The cell and its door were constructed of heavy iron bars.   The large open area outside the cells in the basement contained two desks. A guard dozed at one.

The prison looked impregnable, but anything was possible.

I hope that whatever that 'anything' is, it will arrive damn soon, he thought.

Harvey had been briefed by Jake Glenn, the top CIA man in Thailand, known to his fellow agents as the chief of station.   Then Harvey had parachuted into Laos and trekked into what once had been called South Vietnam.

Harvey had located the Soviet space transmitter he had been sent to find and had gathered the information his CIA superiors wanted. He had radioed the information to Bangkok. Then he set out to investigate more thoroughly to see if he could answer the question of the laser capabilities of the Russian facility. He especially wanted to know if it was equipped to destroy satellites with laser beams.

Harvey knew that capability to shoot down intercontinental missiles was not important in this location, but American communications could be seriously disrupted if satellites were destroyed.

Harvey knew that once he had told his captors about his mission to find the Russian space transmitter they would eliminate him.

Where the hell were his buddies, Jake and some of his friends? he wondered. Harvey could not understand why some word of his CIA associates had not reached him. Surely they must know he had been captured and were well aware of the pressures he was bearing? He knew the Vietnamese would not kill him, on purpose, until he had told them why he was in Vietnam.

He was hungry. He thought of the wonderful long loaves of French bread that had been one of the legacies left by the French colonialists in their ninety-two years of occupation of the country, which ended in 1954. Profits from rubber and rice had created the most gentle of cultures.

Supper arrived, a slice of moldy French bread and a battered tin cup of fetid water. Between the lack of food and dysentery brought on by the unclean water, Harvey had lost forty or fifty pounds.

They gave him just enough food to keep him alive. Harvey was sorely tempted, if something did not happen soon, to tell the Vietnamese enough of what they wanted to know so they would kill him.

Reaction to torture was as varied as the types of torture and the individual undergoing the pain.

The stoic American in the Bastille in Dalat was unwilling to comply with any requests. He bore the pain in silence and often fantasized to avoid the anguish brought on by the horror and the pain.

Americans and English were well known for their resistence to torture. They resorted to several devices, such as fantasizing, to avoid speaking the words their interrogators wanted to hear. Other nationalities, especially the Asiatic, gave in quickly. This was especially true of the Vietnamese, who were routinely tortured as a part of the interrogation process during the Vietnam war. They sought to find what the tormentors wanted them to say and said it quickly, whether true or not.

The method of torture varied from country to country. The Arabs used beating with palm stalks, stoning, or cutting off hands.

The Asiatics were known for their infamous water torture used by the Japanese in World War II. But the Asians borrowed the tearing off of the captive's nails, the electric cattle prod and burning with cigarette stubs from the so-called civilized nations.

Outside the somber gray Bastille, nature was

engaging in a show of beauty that contrasted with the horror in the prison.

North of Dalat the fading day cast its last rays upon the towering mountain, highlighting the green pines on the slopes.

Famous for their strawberries, carrots and giant heads of juicy lettuce and cabbage, Dalat gardeners had ceased the day's labors and shouldered their hoes and rakes. They walked from the communal garden plots to their small, clean, white homes in the outskirts of the city where supper awaited them.   To the west, in the central mountains of Vietnam, the shafts of sunset were as iridescent as an opal. Such a palette in the sky was not a frequent sight in Dalat where storm clouds and rain prevailed most of the year.

Dalat, a sparkling, clean city in the mountains a hundred miles northeast of Saigon, was built around the turn of the century by French rubber plantation owners from the Mekong delta.   These French colonials used the five thousand foot elevation and the cool mountain air for vacations to escape the heat and humidity of the Saigon lowland.

French colonial houses and smaller cottages of red brick and of white and gray stone quarried from the nearby mountains, flanked the wide, tree lined streets.

Halfway around the world, in the Oval Office of the White House, three men were engaged in serious conversation. One was President Ralph Sprague.

"Cameron," the President said, "what about this report on Zimmerman?"

"We think it is accurate, Mr. President," said Cameron Heathcote, Director of Central Intelligence. "Zimmerman is the lone agent in Vietnam on Project Dragon. I know he located the Soviet space transmitter, but I know nothing else except he has been captured and probably identified.

"I have brought my deputy director for operations, Hamilton Campbell, with me to give you direct answers and to discuss our problem of rescuing Zimmerman.

"Earlier we discussed whether to recommend to you sending in by helicopter a SWAT team of eight or ten men highly trained in explosives and small arms. We decided the best way would be a solo operation by one competent man to enhance secrecy and prevent disclosure of American involvement."

The Director reported he had approached two different men in the agency, but both had exercised their right to decline a highly dangerous task. After some discussion, the President agreed with the Director to call up a qualified man from retirement, Ulysses McCutcheon, if he would accept the task.

McCutcheon was one of the intelligence officers trained in clandestine operations who had retired just before the shit hit the fan and America pulled out of Vietnam. Later developments made him happy he had retired at fifty-five years of age. He was not at all pleased when Cameron Heathcote was made Director two years later and began swinging his ax at some of Lyss's friends to reduce the size of the clandestine service, and, as Heathcote said publicly, to get his own people in control.

After retirement McCutcheon had moved to West Virginia to a timber farm he had bought during his working years.

"Mr. President, he is a good man. He had an exceptional war record. In one behind the lines mission in France, he recaptured an armored personnel carrier and came back in it with five prisoners and key intelligence information. He got the Distinguished Service Cross for that, to add to one he had already been awarded in Italy. He is a solid, hard worker. He has the excellent imagination required of a good clandestine operator. He is still in fine physical condition. To accomplish this task, he will need brains, strength, endurance and lot of luck," Hamilton Campbell said.

"I know him personally and quite well."

"Even though Campbell has recommended him to me," the Director said. "I really would rather have someone else, preferably from our active officers. As Campbell has pointed out to me, there is a security advantage in using McCutcheon, who has been out of sight for three years. He knows Vietnam intimately. He served in Saigon when Campbell was top CIA man there."

"I am told he does not like me because I retired some of his friends. But he has an excessively strong feeling of patriotism. If he can be convinced it is best for the country, Campbell and I both believe he will do it.

"Mr. President, it appears you agree with us on running it as a solo operation, rather than a batch of helicopters and some gung-ho Marines."

"Yes, I do. Have Campbell get in touch with McCutcheon. Don't do it yourself. Then, if you can get him in town, make it Wednesday. I'm having dinner that night at the Langdorf's out in northwest Washington. Surely a secret meeting can be set up in the backyard or somewhere close."

"But, Mr. President," the Director said, "he's not fond of you either, primarily because you are the one who appointed me."

"You say he has an excessively strong feeling of patriotism. Can he resist a request from the President of the country he loves, even if he doesn't love the President?"

"You are, of course, right, sir," the Director said. "I will have Campbell get in touch with him and make the arrangements."

DRAGONS YET TO SLAY

CHAPTER TWO

Colonel Ulysses McCutcheon sat at his desk in a large upstairs room of a farm home in the West Virginia mountains.

In Lyss's career in international espionage, one of his great advantages had been that he was not obvious in a crowd. His opponents in the intelligence business could not pick him out of the group, as was the case with some other intelligence officers.

Those who knew Lyss knew he was an intense, vibrant man with a good mind and good physical coordination, both of which had saved his life on more than one occasion.

His straight-combed, dark brown hair had a few streaks of gray in it. His nose was acquiline. His eyes gray. He was brown from the spring sun on his face. He certainly did not look like a World War II hero, which he was, having been awarded the Distinguished Service Cross twice, once in Italy for leading a patrol across the Volturno River and again in the Colmar pocket of Eastern France.

His father had often said, "Lyss was born with two left feet, and he always gets them tangled up."

He was clumsy on the dance floor, but agile and competent on the tennis court.

Some of Lyss's old spy friends said if he was like anything it was an old shoe with a hole in the sole. Upon being ribbed about such a comparison, Lyss had laughed and recalled one of the famous political campaign pictures, showing Adlai Stevenson's feet on a desk, exposing a hole in his shoe.

"Being called one of Adlai's old shoes ain't bad at all."

He had bought this farm in Randolph County, West Virginia, ten years ago. He had enjoyed trips to the farm and supervising the renovation of the home whenever he could get time away from Washington.

Upon his retirement three years ago, in early 1975, Lyss and his wife, Mathilda, had moved to the farm. He had continued improving the place, and the house, to include this study.

He had covered the walls with the paraphenalia of his career. There were pictures of professional associates, of family and of friends, many autographed. On one wall was a large U.S. Air Force Physical-Political Chart of the World, with pencil marks of Lyss's travels. It was the focus of attraction to visitors. The map was centered on the North Pole, which had upset one of his Australian friends.

"Typical prejudice against the southern hemisphere."

Lyss had responded that only five of his world trips in thirty years had been south of the equator.

Lyss paused in front of the picture of General Chandler Boone, who had pinned the Legion of Merit on Lyss in Vietnam.

The general had said, "This Legion of Merit doesn't hold candle to the Distinguished Service Cross you got in Europe, but it is the best I can give you here in Vietnam."

Lyss had said, "As I recall, sir, you got the DSC in Europe yourself, as well as several other medals. If I may be permitted to say so, sir, I feel you earned your medals more than I earned mine."

Lyss had a great admiration for Boone, the same size as Lyss, perhaps a bit stockier. A cigar was always present. General Boone had died in Washington about the time Lyss got back from Vietnam.

He mused in front of his mother's picture, recalling how she was filled with love, which she lavished on her children, especially Lyss. She had agreed to her Yankee father-in-law naming the last of her sons Ulysses Grant McCutcheon. Then she laughed when Lyss named his son Robert Lee. Lyss said it evened out the score between the Blue and the Gray.

Lyss paused before the last picture taken of his Victorian father, a history teacher in Davis and Elkins

College.

"To use profanity is to profess your ignorance of the English language. If you feel you must have some sort of expletive, say Boulder. That's the biggest dam in the world," his father had often said.

Lyss had always respected his stern father. *Maybe feared is closer to the truth*, he thought.

His father was one of those old fashioned people who thought it was not manly to show emotion publicly.

Lyss smiled as he recalled one of those rare moments with his father where emotion reigned. He had come home from the university with a personal problem—at the moment Lyss could not remember what the problem had been—and he expected a tongue-lashing from his father.

Instead, with tears in his eyes, the older man had taken his son into his arms and embraced him, consoling him with carefully chosen words.

Lyss had returned to the university to get his degree and his ROTC commission.

Still smiling with pleasure over one of the few times his father had demonstrated his love, Lyss left the study. He went down to the front porch, where he was welcomed by his daughter, Constance. She had anticipated his arrival and offered him a scotch and water.

He sat on the porch, looking east at Cheat Mountain and the hardwood trees beginning to leaf out, with a few pines spotted throughout the forest to add extra green. The trees on top of the mountains were still stark and bare from the winter.

Lyss recalled the late spring when he had joined some sheep raisers in an effort to hunt down a killer bear in that tangled area. The eastern mountains of West Virginia varied greatly from the well groomed, carefully harvested woods on Lyss's farm. In the high mountains there was thick growth, almost junglelike in its tangled brush. Dense thickets of beautiful laurel in bloom predominated. Laurel was one of the most beautiful flowers of the mountains. The hunters found the laurel almost impossible to get through. Tall red oak trees spread their branches over much of the land. The white and pink blossoms of the laurel flourished beneath both oak and pines.

Clayton Walker, one of the farmers whose sheep had been mauled by the bear, was successful in hitting the animal with his Winchester .375.

"I know I got him good," he said. The bear struggled into the dense laurel and was never found.

That winter Lyss twice had nightmares about the bear. Lyss was standing in a clearing, and the great bear charged out of the laurel at him, blood coming from a chest wound and his mouth. Lyss had awakened from the dreams with a jolt, sweating heavily.

Casting his previous thoughts aside, he turned his mind to his daughter, Connie, seated beside him.

After Connie had been widowed, she had come

out to the farm to visit and recover from the death of her captain husband in the final days of Saigon. She stayed in West Virginia because she was needed to teach in the Valley Head Elementary School where her love was poured out on young children she had never had an opportunity to bear.

With the death of her mother, Lyss had asked her if she could take over running the household. He was startled by her reply.

"No, but I can help. If we can get someone to keep the house clean, with your help, we can make a go of it."

At the funeral and the traumatic days that followed, his daughter had been his staunch supporter. She knew his grief was mixed with relief because of Mathilda's long terminal illness.

Breaking the silence and his thoughts, the telephone rang.

Lyss returned to the porch a few minutes later.

"Hamilton Campbell wants to meet me in that restaurant in Georgetown called the Rive Gauche Wednesday at seven-thirty. He says it is strictly business and a meeting will follow dinner."

Timing was not essential to Lyss's meeting with Hamilton Campbell, but old habits were hard to break. Lyss entered the restaurant at exactly 7:30.

Ham was at one of the booths over at the right. The Rive Gauche was a plush, spacious, well upholstered restaurant.

Lyss walked over to Ham's booth and sat down.

He felt there was no need to be clandestine, but his years of training had taught him there was no need to invite attention, either.

As they neared the end of the meal, and as Lyss savored the last few drops of wine, Ham laughed.

"For a West Virginia hillbilly, you've picked up a lot of continental joys in your travels."

They did not discuss business during dinner. Lyss had not expected them to. Ham had said there would be a separate meeting after dinner. Lyss knew the meeting would be in some safe place.

Lyss's health was a topic in which Ham seemed keenly interested. Were his lungs okay again? Had he had a recent X-ray. Did it show the clot completely absorbed? Happily, Lyss reported that for a man in his late fifties all was well.

"I get a bit tired after three sets of tennis, but that's West Virginia mountain air for you."

They sipped their coffee. Ham said, "Where is your car?"

"Parked by the valet."

"Okay, get it, circle the block. Put it in that all night parking lot on M Street. You know where I mean?"

"Yes."

"Cross over M Street, then walk west, and a Yellow Cab will stop. A girl you will recognize will say, 'Looking for a taxi, mister?' Take it."

Lyss felt a bit of exhilaration. So it was to be a really secret meeting. These were unusual precautions. He wondered if it would be in one of the old safe houses downtown. He wondered what it was all about and where it would lead. His long training showed. He asked no questions. The case officer—and in this situation that was precisely what Ham was —must have complete and unquestioned control. There would be a time and a place for questions.

Lyss's years of training in the intelligence profession had taught him the necessity of timing, of synchronizing watches and actions. If Lyss, as case officer, arranged to pick up an agent on the street, the agent and the case officer compared the time as shown on their watches. The agent was told to arrive, walking at a normal pace, not loitering, at the middle of the pickup block at precisely the right time. The case officer arrived at that point at exactly the same moment. The pickup was accomplished smoothly and quickly.

Another type of such coordination was the one Lyss was now expected to accomplish. Ham, as the case officer, dispatched Lyss on his errand, estimating the time required from leaving the restaurant until the taxi pickup point.

Lyss did as instructed. As he hit the right spot on M Street, a Yellow Cab came to a stop by him.

"Looking for a cab, mister?"

When Lyss slipped into the backseat of the taxi, he got a pleasant surprise.

"Hello, Sally darlin'," he said.

"Maybe Sarah darling, but knock off that hillbilly accent and the Sally bit."

"Hello, you Connecticut Yankee."

"Hello, you West Virginia hillbilly."

Five years had elapsed since Lyss and Sarah Sanford had served together in Vietnam. They had never worked in the same office together. Although Lyss was a senior officer, he never was her direct supervisor. They had met socially, liked each other from the beginning. A close friendship developed.

The American presence in Vietnam was, by its military nature, predominantly, overwhelmingly, male. There was a time when the wives of key officers were permitted in country, but it was an unusual thing.

In Vietnam, Lyss and Sarah had not been lovers. She had often served as Lyss's hostess at dinners he gave there for high level visiting Americans and for Vietnamese officials.

Living in Saigon villas with French trained cooks, the most common social event was dinner. Even the senior officials present without wives liked having female company at the dinner table. When the honored guests were Vietnamese, they often preferred to bring their wives. Under such circumstances, an American hostess was highly desirable.

Most of the American women stationed in Vietnam, like Sarah, lived in Saigon. In rural areas, villages were sometimes overrun by the Viet Cong. Even in Saigon there were occasional rocket attacks.

The car turned off Foxhall Road onto Nebraska Avenue, then they turned off Nebraska into one of the nicer residential areas of Washington. Lyss had always marvelled at the beauty of the nation's capital. He usually conveniently forgot about the slums east of the capitol.

The taxi stopped at a large, two story, colonial style, white clapboard house. There were no cars parked there. One light was on over the front door.

Lyss paid the taxi. With Sarah on his arm, he went into the house. She turned on the living room lights. The windows facing the street displayed the two to public view, if there were any passersby. Sarah poured two drinks. They sat down.

She looked at her watch.

"Thirteen minutes. When I tell you, we will stroll to the back door. There is a brick walk to a back gate. Go through. Ten steps straight ahead and turn right and you will see a little servant's cottage of the old fashioned variety. You remember servants? You remember how life was with them,"

It really was the first time she seemed to relax.

She had that old teasing expression in her gray-green eyes. It added to her loveliness.

At the appointed time, Lyss took the walk. It was a clear, crisp night. Unconsciously, he counted the steps, even though it was not really necessary. He was in a well groomed, rear garden of a large home. Sounds of music and gaiety came from the big house.

He turned right and entered the cottage. It had a small living room with the usual couch and two chairs, a television, and some end tables. A trim, conservatively dressed young man rose from the couch as Lyss entered.

"Colonel M?" he asked. Upon acknowledgement, he asked Lyss to sit down. "Let me see your driver's license," he said.

Now, Lyss thought, *how damned silly can you get*? How many characters were going to walk through that back gate into this yard with a big party going on in the house up front and enter this cottage so confidently?

Lyss shrugged his shoulders and showed his driver's license. The security man then handed Lyss a laminated card with a thumbprint under the plastic.

"Press your right thumb there." He pointed.

Lyss did. The security officer made a quick, but thorough comparison. Then he turned and left the room.

In a few minutes there was someone at the door. It was a lone man. He entered and Lyss restrained a gasp.

It was the President of the United States!

CHAPTER THREE

"Harvey Zimmerman is alive."

The President had blurted out the statement, which was almost as startling to Lyss as the President's presence.

In the first place, Lyss had no idea where Zimmerman was and what he was working on. Three years away from the "pickle factory" had left him no access to classified information.

The President explained that Zimmerman had been dispatched on a mission into South Vietnam, had provided some information about a Soviet installation there, but was captured as he sought further data. He was, the President disclosed, in prison in Dalat as of ten days ago.

"And I want you to go in and get him. Normally, a request of this type would come to you from the Director, but I am asking you to do this dangerous task because I have been told you do not like the Director I appointed. I have been told you are one of the few men competent enough to do the job, which is essential to our national security."

The tall man seated himself and lit up a cigar, which he puffed thoughtfully. Lyss was thinking, as the President paused, that he, Ulysses McCutcheon, was living a page of history, a page that would never be made public. The President was not Lyss's choice, but he was the President of the United States and a world figure.

Lyss felt that when his time came to speak, in view of the momentous occasion, he must choose his words carefully.

"Indeed," the President said, "I have been told that you do not like me, either. I am President of the country I know you love. Your years of service are proof enough of that. This task is immensely important.

"I know you have laid your life on the line in three wars. I suspect your life with the spooks has not been dull.

"Are you still prepared to die for your country and for the rescue of a CIA compatriot? It will be a really dangerous mission. We may wind up losing both you and Zimmerman. He has intimate knowledge of Project Dragon. Our monitoring of the Vietnamese clearly indicates he has not disclosed anything yet. How long can he withstand severe interrogation?

"He is alive and we want him home."

Lyss replied in measured, carefully controlled

tones, leaving no doubt of their truth.

"The older I get the stronger is my understanding of the mortality of man. I am a mortal man. The more years that pass by, the less I worry about it. I guess, Mr. President, you could say I am old enough to die.

"I would rather die for a good purpose, if death is one of the risks of that purpose, than to await "the cruel disintegration of the slow years", as Doctor Hans Zinsser, the famous medical missionary to the Philippines, put it."*

"I take that," the President said, "as a tentative yes. It is an honor to meet you. Wait five minutes and go back the way you came. I wish you luck."

Sarah was waiting when Lyss returned. She had a whimsical, querulous smile that said she was terribly curious about what the President of the United States would want with him. Additionally, Lyss felt she was intensely proud. She was also a professional in the intelligence business, so she asked no questions.

"You may now accept a free drink at Chez Sarah," she said, "and get that gleam out of your eye. There is work yet to do tonight."

---

*"As I Remember Him". Little, Brown & Co., 1940

Lyss mused over their relationship during those two years that they had become such good friends. She was then, and now, an attractive woman. Lyss's private thoughts dwelled on two things. The first was his delight at seeing an old friend. The second was that it had been two years since Mattie died, and some time before that since he had taken a woman to bed.

Looking at her, Lyss thought what pleasure a night in bed with her would bring him, and he hoped, her.

Vietnam's permissive society, the atmosphere of battle and sense of mortality had brought many Americans to share the same bed, whether married or not. The readily available Vietnamese women were the common bedfellows with American men.

Sarah's refusal to spend the night with Lyss brought on their first fight. After a lobster dinner at his home in Saigon one night, they had several increasingly hot kisses.

"Why go back to your place? Spend the night here with me," he said.

She had recoiled violently.

"No. No. Damn it, I knew you'd get around to spoiling a perfectly good friendship one time or another."

He had taken her to her quarters that night. She

had refused to see him for two weeks, then they met at a party in the apartment of Catherine Smith, a mutual friend. Lyss approached her, smiling and apologetic.

"Let's be friends. I'll keep my pants buttoned."

She had agreed.

Now, in the car, Lyss looked at her profile. Her skin was still smooth. Her nose had a slight perk to it. She had a solid but not too prominent chin. The years had added to her appeal, he thought.

She had anticipated the schedule. A taxi was waiting out front. It was a short trip to a massive cliff of apartments on Massachusetts Avenue. They soon were in a spacious, tastefully decorated apartment.

The focal point of the living room was a large, overstuffed divan, long enough for even the tall Ham Campbell to lie on.

An Indian brass tray on wooden legs served as the coffee table. An Arab gawa pot, used to make coffee over a campfire, still stained with the smoke of desert fires, was on the coffee table. Three magazines, *U.S. News and World Report, Time*, and *Newsweek* were there. The ruffled pages, with a tear here and there, indicated all three had been well read.

A matching overstuffed chair was at right angles to the divan. At one wall was a small teak portable bar Lyss knew had come from Denmark.

Framed pictures on the wall varied from an oil painting of the Colorado mountains to a Japanese scroll. There were mementoes from Lebanon, Germany, Kenya and the inevitable ceramic elephant from Vietnam.

It was the apartment of a professional person who had toured much of the world, and who had a taste for the good things of life, especially those pleasing to the eye.

Lyss knew it had been a financial struggle for Sarah to finish at the University of Connecticut. She was interviewed by the CIA and was delighted to accept their offer to become a special trainee.

Sometimes, when she and Lyss were together in their early days in Vietnam, they engaged in recollections of past thoughts and desires. She had said that being a professional and living alone was not always the happy life. She had missed the normal woman's life with marriage and children. But she liked her career.

"Of course," she had said, "it would be good to hold a little hand in mine."

The large window of her apartment overlooked a good portion of Washington with Memorial Bridge in the distance.

The dining nook, with its walnut table and four chairs, was in the far corner with picture windows. In the distance loomed the massive capitol.

A door to the left of the living room led into a small, efficient kitchen, sparkling white and trimmed in blue. The kitchen was also open at the end toward the dining nook.

Hamilton Campbell was in the apartment waiting for them. Lyss was delighted to see him again. He had been the Chief of the CIA Station during most of Lyss's stay there.

"Lyss, there's a hell of a lot of danger. It may be an impossible mission, but I think you have a good chance of pulling it off. As lucky as you are, you have faced danger before and come away from it. The real question is: will you give up that damned rocking chair on your front porch and take on a job for your country that's terribly important?

"The detailed information we hope Harvey has may be a vital key to negotiations the President is about to launch with the Russians. It will damage his efforts if the Soviets find out why we sent a spy into one of their front yards."

Lyss could feel the adrenaline flowing, the surge of strength and the joy of anticipation of combat.

Lyss loved his country. Often tears had flowed from his eyes at the playing of the national anthem. He took off his hat and placed it over his heart as the flag paraded by. Lyss was angered to see hippies spit on the flag and sickened to see some protesters burn it.

"I am not impressed that that intellectual idiot the admiral wants me to do something, or that wimp of a president, either.   I strongly suspect others were asked to do the job and either said no or were too scared to do it."

Lyss was almost snarling.

"Now, level with me, what do you and Sarah think about the job and me as the goat heading for slaughter? What you have to say means a lot to me."

Suddenly, across his mind came a memory of his son, Bobby Lee, who, as a boy, had turned to him one day and said, "Dad, what is a coward and what is a brave man?"

Lyss had replied that both trembled when faced with danger, but the brave man overcame the nervousness and went on to do his duty.

He resumed his conversation with Ham, pointing out he had faced his share of peril. With a wife dead and two children grown, there was only himself to consider.

"A guy who says he doesn't fear death," Lyss said, "is either an idiot or a damned liar. I'd lots rather die for a genuine cause than be run over by some drunk in a car."

Ham said it was the answer he had expected.

"The job has its pitfalls and dangers. I would be less than honest with you if I did not tell you that two current employees have been asked to do the job. They have exercised their right to refuse a high risk task. The job is extremely important. I recommended you to the Director.

"Whether you are in love with the President or not doesn't really make a damn."

Ham smirked as he said that.

"What is important is whether you are willing, as I said in the beginning, to give up the ease and comfort of your farm to take on a job that, literally, might be your last one. That is why I asked my first question."

Lyss was not surprised at Ham's words. He had figured the task would be unusual and difficult. Myriad questions flashed across his mind.

First, should he give up the quiet, good life that he was living in the beautiful mountains of West Virginia?

Then his thoughts turned to his grandchildren, and his son, Bobby Lee, and daughter, Connie. As they grew up, they came to expect their father to leave home for faraway places.   Lyss thought it was not really fair to the kids, but admitted to himself that Mattie had done well in raising the family.

Now it was different. They were stable in life and not leaning on a father or mother for anything.

Lyss recalled how his advice and influence had helped Bobby Lee get his act in order after the Elkins Haberdashery, a men's clothing store, had gone broke.

Bobby Lee, who had always loved dogs and cats, then moved to Washington. With Lyss's help, he had set up a pet shop that was now doing well.

"I guess, Dad," Bobby Lee had said, "I was meant to sell little kittens."

Instead of such mundane family history, perhaps he should be thinking that within weeks or months those grandkids would be weeping over an urn of ashes, assuming his body could be brought back.

It took but a moment for these thoughts to pass through his mind.

He turned to Ham. There was genuine concern in his face.

DRAGONS YET TO SLAY

CHAPTER FOUR

"What the hell has Zimmerman got himself into? When he goes off half cocked, he doesn't have enough sense to pour piss out of a boot," Lyss said.

"Well, I've already given you the highlights," Ham said. "By the way, we've insured security on conversations here tonight. We've used Sarah's place before. The security boys went over it today, checking for listening devices. Even the phone is unplugged.

"I have a piece of business to finish before we go on with our talk."

He turned to Sarah, his height towering over her.

"You probably have already put two and two together, but this is to inform you officially that Lyss has been asked by the Director and the President to undertake a dangerous mission. You will now be the sixth person to know the details of that task.

"This project is highly classified. A minimum number of people will be involved. I want you to be case officer during the training period.

"If you will volunteer to stay with it, I'd like for you to be case officer for the entire project.

"No one is to be given a hint of this job, except on my approval, which will be subject to Lyss's recommendations and our joint agreement."

"The task involves a high risk solo rescue from Vietnam.

"I thought it would be something special," Sarah said, "but I didn't know it would be so dangerous. It's not only dangerous, but foolish, if I'm reading you correctly. How in God's name do either of you think one man, operating alone, can pull off a rescue operation in enemy territory?"

Ham did not reply, but turned to Lyss and briefed him on Project Dragon and Zimmerman's part in it, closing with the latest report that Harvey was in prison in Dalat.

Then they discussed Lyss being well known in Vietnam, where probably the most knowledgeable of the Vietnamese had identified him as CIA. Campbell added the defector Abel had confirmed the Soviets had a file on Ulysses McCutcheon.

"So you know damned well that the Vietnamese either know it or can get it mighty easily, as close as the Soviets are to the new regime of Vietnam.

"For these reasons, we feel if you accept the task, you must publicly die and be given a new identity.

"I had thought maybe an accident on one of your mountain roads en route home. You have a reputation for fast driving.   Too much speed on one of your mountain curves would be ample excuse. We can arrange for an oncoming car to make it genuine.

"You know that route better than any of us and can recommend a spot for the accident.

"You've always said you intended to be cremated, if somebody could find the body in whatever remote corner of the globe you die. Cremation will remove the last traceable identification of the body we use, which, by the way, is an unclaimed body from a local morgue that otherwise would be buried in Potter's Field.

"I understand you've requested the ashes be spread on the mountain above your farm home.

"We have the surgeon and the technique to alter your appearance. In our discussions, we thought it might be best if you became a Filipino."

Lyss's first thoughts were on the difficulties of facial surgery, which he had never undergone. Then he recognized that a Filipino would be more likely than any other foreigner to be welcomed in the new Vietnam. *I have always liked the Filipinos, and I think they have liked me.*

Ham turned.

"Maybe I'm jumping the gun, although I certainly don't think so. Will you accept the task? You may die in the mountains of Vietnam, or you may rescue a man who is important to our way of life. If his captors learn of his mission, and especially if they get him to tell what he knows, it may endanger current negotiations and relations with the Soviets."

"Sorry to use an old Mafia movie cliche," Lyss said, "but I've been made an offer that I can't refuse."

Ham smirked. *Mafia* was not a popular word in the agency. An early effort to get Mafia support in bringing down Castro had been one of the Agency's most publicized failures.

Lyss smiled as he said it, but hoped he looked as deadly serious as he felt.

"I need to think a few minutes before we continue this talk. This is not only a matter of danger, but a matter of practicality. Can it be done? By me? By anyone? In a matter of only a few minutes, I'm being asked to volunteer for what may very well be my last trip abroad.

"You and Sarah discuss administrative details a while. I'll go out on the balcony and look at the stars, even if they aren't as pretty as my West Virginia ones."

Standing on the balcony with his hands on the rail, Lyss looked up at the sky. Unusual for Washington, Lyss saw most of the stars of the universe.

Diverse thought passed rapidly through his mind, like changing television channels in search of a program. Lyss realized he was about to undertake a dangerous and unusual challenge. Then he remembered entering the intelligence business in the first place because of the challenge, the intensity, the unusual nature of the work.

He wondered if the cosmetic surgery would be painful, then his thoughts dwelt on whether his face could be returned to normal or would be permanently altered.

Lyss did not think for a minute that he was being cocksure or overconfident with his strong feeling that he would succeed. It would be a major achievement, certainly different from the routine life of sorrows and happiness he had led for the past three years.

Lyss had left Elkins, West Virginia, for the state university in 1936, with the dual aim of a college degree and an Army commission through the ROTC. He excelled and was granted a Regular Army commission as a Distinguished Military Cadet in 1940. He served in the Third Infantry Division and was three times decorated, twice with the Distinguished Service Cross, once in Italy and once in France.

When the war was over in Europe, Lyss volunteered for China because he planned to remain in the regular army. He thought he would have some weeks, perhaps even months, in the states before shipping out to the Pacific. Waiting for him was a wife and a three-year-old daughter he hardly knew. He hoped for some good time with them before returning to combat.

He did not know that he had volunteered for the OSS. It required additional training. He would happy to have Mattie and Connie right with him.

Then the atomic bomb ended the war.

In later years Lyss often wondered why he stayed in the intelligence business as it was folding up. He concluded that the challenges would be in intelligence in peacetime.

General Donovan, himself about to leave, told Lyss there soon would be some sort of central intelligence apparatus. He had been right. It was organized as the CIA in 1947 and incorporated the bits and pieces of what was left of OSS.

Enough of that sort of thinking, Lyss told himself. He felt he had now agreed to work and live with a strong threat of death. He had never been one to hesitate on a decision. Sometimes in the past his superiors had criticized him for snap judgments.

He smiled, thinking of the times he had had to decide quickly and that he had been right most of the time. If the enemy was coming at him with an AK-47 pointed at his belly, he did not have a great deal of time to decide what to do. He had been wrong often enough to stay honest.

Lyss's thoughts momentarily replaced the highly emotional atmosphere of the past hour. Currently most people his age lived in the past. Lyss was happy to enjoy the present and anticipate the coming years.

Perhaps in recent times, he had been more inclined to live in the past than his professed desire of living in the present and anticipating tomorrow. He knew this new future was for him. A short future, maybe, but he was cocky enough to believe he could pull it off.

So he turned his mind to the problem, to the tasks that must be done, the people he might need and the equipment that would help. He found some answers and some questions.

At last, Lyss was ready to return to the conversation.

"Lyss, I didn't see you bowing toward Mecca or even lighting any joss sticks," Sarah said. Smiling, she handed Lyss a scotch on the rocks. He added a splash of water.

"Okay," he said, as they sat around the Indian brass tray, which was Sarah's coffee table.

"First, of course I'll take on this job. You knew that before you asked me. Although Harvey and I were never really friends, we were closely associated a couple of times. I don't want to let a CIA employee rot in jail. Most important is to get him out of there before he tells them something significant. It's nice to know it will serve a national purpose. We'll discuss the details later after you've given me all the information you have.

"To address the reservations expressed by Sarah, let me say I think the only way this task can be done without revealing the American hand in it, is to have a singleton operation."

Lyss pointed out that, although he would be

operating alone, there were certainly some Vietnamese who might be persuaded to assist without getting any details of what Lyss was up to.   They agreed on the security of the project. It must be more tightly held than most projects.

Then Lyss said the case officer would be able to cover a lot of requests and turn back a lot of questions. He hoped Sarah would be the case officer.

Sarah spoke up. "Both of you know me better than to doubt my answer. Of course, I'll accept."

She was right. There never was any doubt in Lyss's mind that she would take on the job and carry out her duties in a professional manner. He continued.

"I want one outsider to know my death is staged, not real, and that, God willing, I shall return. That's Connie.

"If I don't return, I want a very special favor. I want the President to call my daughter and son into a private meeting and tell them I did not die in an asinine automobile accident, but in a foreign country in the service of our country.

"No particulars would need to be given, but I think eventually, when they can be told, I would like my grandkids to know the old man was a patriot, even if a foolish one.

"Maybe it's some sort of kharma or massive egotism or whatever, but there are those who see our immortality as being lived out in our descendents.

"Anyway, I want those kids to know someday

that Granddaddy tried his best to serve this country well.

"There are several reasons why I'm undertaking this task, and not the least of them is that I do love our country intensely. You understand that, Ham."

They discussed briefing Connie. After some objection, Ham agreed to it.

"Now," Lyss said, "what details do you have about Harvey and his captors?"

"Ten days ago he was in Dalat," Ham said. "He's in solitary confinement in what used to be an old French army *caserne*. You may remember the building. While our source did not see him close enough to talk to him, he's positive it's Harvey and he's in questionable health. He has lost quite a bit of weight. Our source said the Vietnamese were unhappy they had not been able to get him to talk."

"Well," Lyss said, "as big as that rascal is a few pounds loss would not weaken him too much, but a severe loss might add to the problem of moving him to safety. I'm sure he talked a lot to his Vietnamese captors, but didn't really tell them anything. That's his way of doing things."

Lyss recalled the old building at the south edge of Dalat with its somber, gray stone. He and his American associates had called it the Bastille in the late sixties.

Ham continued the discussion by again pointing out that Lyss was too well known to take on this task without an elaborate disguise.

"That is why we feel you must die and a new identity be provided. I've suggested Filipino, but we want to hear your ideas, too."

Lyss agreed and expressed hope the tech boys could make him look like a Filipino. Among his language capabilities was a working knowledge of Tagalog, good French, good Spanish, and satisfactory Vietnamese.

"Of course," Ham said, "you'll have some time to brush up on languages. The tech boys have injections that will change your skin pigment for about six months. The plastic surgeons will have to do the rest."

"Okay," Lyss said. "Now some general thoughts on personnel. As I drove over here, I did some speculating. A lot of it seems to have been on target. ESP, I guess. Anyway, I was hoping that if I have to have some help, we might check with some of the other old ducks and see if they want a challenge and some risk. I'll have to be single in the country because you can't put several guys together on this kind of mission. It's risky enough for a single, but I'll have to have some support and excellent communicaions.

"I had a Christmas card from Alfred and Antoinette Bennett from Ruratonga in the South Pacific, which I gather is their home base, but I get occasional cards from odd corners as they sail the *Pharaon* into faraway corners of the world. Are you in touch with Al?"

Ham looked amused.

"You never did miss a trick, you clever bastard. We implemented the project you and Al wrote up several years ago. When he retired, we took him on to move around in those exotic areas where normal contact either does not exist or is so fleeting we cannot cover it economically.

"Yes, I'm in touch with Al. He could be spared, if he is willing."

"Well, this whole damned thing is voluntary, isn't it?"

"Yep. I'll find out if he will volunteer. If he knows it is you, he will. He told me once you saved his life in Pleiku."

"Bullshit, of course. It was more like he saved mine. Anyway, we have been blessed with a strong and abiding friendship. Moreover, his years at sea have made him tops in the sailing line."

Then Al's other professional capabilities were discussed, including that he was one of the fastest Morse code operators in the Agency.

"Of course," Lyss said, "we use voice transmissions now, protected by squirt, condensing a one minute message into six seconds.

"I will need to talk turkey with some of the tech boys, or get somebody who can. Joshua Rosenbloom has retired, hasn't he? He was one of the best gadget men I've ever known."

"Yes," Ham said. "Josh has a place near the water in Maine and an antenna that reaches halfway to the moon. He spends most of his time hamming it up on the air. I suspect he would appreciate a few months of diversion."

"That's the whole idea, Ham. I'm not questioning the capabilities of your current crop of bright young turks in the agency, but it's my idea to use retired guys when we can. We might increase the security and certainly lessen the profile of the project by using us old ducks rather than your young bloods.

"Josh has an additional advantage, too. He's a good gun man. He fixed up a Browning 9mm handgun for me in India once, and even I could hit something with it."

They agreed that other requirements would come up as the work progressed.

Then they discussed money, with Ham pointing out that they were amply funded, but they could not be as free with money as in the golden days of the fifties and sixties.

"You'll have all you need," Ham said, "and that includes compensation, which we've not mentioned."

Lyss was not reluctant to talk personal money, but it really seemed off the subject in a way.

"I figured we will get all expenses and no problem. Additional pay had not occurred to me. I guess some is in line. You set that up as you see fit. We'll abide by it."

"Now," Ham said, "this funeral we have arranged has to be pretty soon. We have a body on hand
that won't keep forever.

"In a limited way, I'm going to bring in one of
my best young security officers. He's the one you met
tonight. He will work with Sarah in staging the wreck
of your car."

They agreed to meet in Sarah's apartment again
at two o'clock the next afternoon to go over other
details, including any new thoughts Lyss might have.

"And now," Ham said, with a sigh, "forgive
me, old friend, but I'm tired. It's nearly two o'clock."

Sarah turned quickly to Ham and said, "You
live well out toward Bethesda. I'll take Lyss to his
car."

"Okay," Ham said. He took Lyss's hand, then
closed his left hand on top of it.

"Thank God for guys like you. I hope your luck
is equal to your courage."

Ham departed. Lyss wearily sat down at the
end of the couch.

Sarah went to the bar and poured two drinks,
then walked over toward Lyss.

"Follow me," she said, smiling. Drinks in
hand, she headed for the bedroom.

Lyss hastily arose and followed her.

DRAGONS YET TO SLAY

CHAPTER FIVE

The bright rays of a spring dawn streamed through the breakfast nook windows. Lyss was sitting at the table with his first cup of coffee when Sarah came in wearing a fluffy robe.

"How about some breakfast, lover," she said.

"Great idea."

Lyss rose and took her into his arms. They said nothing for a moment. Then she kissed him and moved away. She gathered some things from various nooks and crannies of the kitchen, including the refrigerator, and began the breakfast.

Lyss walked up behind her. He put his arms around her waist and nuzzled the back of her neck.

"Get off me, man, if you want breakfast. I can't cook with you hanging on. Go someplace besides the bedroom and slurp your coffee."

She smiled as she said it.

Sarah completed the breakfast and brought in a tray of scrambled eggs, toast and jelly, with two fresh cups of coffee.   She sat down with a contented sigh.

She looked up at Lyss.

"Man, you're good in bed."

She smiled. "I could get used to that."

"I guess I could knock the pins outa Dr. Franco by telling him I know an old duck damned near sixty who can screw like crazy.

"It was nice, Lyss. You are wonderful. You know, of course, that I've always loved you. I kept my distance, and yours, when my ethics told me I had to.

"You're my kind of buccaneer. It doesn't surprise me that you have taken on this job. I fully expect to hear about you someday, going down with your ship with a knife in your teeth and a sword raised high.

"You are a damned fool, you know, but you are my kind of damned fool."

Lyss could see a tear floating down from her eye. He got up and went to her chair, lifting her head as he stooped down.   Softly he kissed the salty cheek, then gave her a full and vigorous kiss on the mouth.

"I doubt if anything we might tell Dr. Franco would surprise that bastard. These past few hours have been wonderful.

She returned to her breakfast. He looked again at this exceptional woman. She simply had not run into the right buccaneer at the right time, Lyss thought. She had focused her life and her energies on a professional career that would have brought greater recognition if she had been a man instead of a woman. She was aware of her femininity, and apparently always had been. But she did not attempt to capitalize on it as Lyss had seen some pretty women do.

During the quiet breakfast, they watched the day's light increase and the mists of the Potomac Valley lift and open the nation's capital for business. She had placed her small dinette table near the window. The vista of Washington to the southeast was inspiring to Lyss. The distant dome of the capitol housed the conglomeration of Americans who combined to serve their country, their districts and their constituency.

Washington had always been special to him, the headquarters from which he had operated for nearly three decades.

Lyss wanted his grandchildren to live in the same freedom, cursing whoever was in power at the time, but rising with insurmountable might against the foes who sought to overthrow it.

"Sarah," Lyss said as his reverie was broken. "I expect the least that is seen of my car in Georgetown the better. How about you dropping me off somewhere near the parking lot? I'll pick my car up. At one o'clock you can pick me up at the Farragut entrance to the club."

At one-thirty Lyss was back in Sarah's apartment to meet Ham, who arrived precisely at two.

"Well, first of all," Ham said, "you'll be interested to know that I talked with Joshua Rosenbloom this morning and he will be with us day after tomorrow at our country location.

"This project is taking over our new estate entirely. We will keep it for the necessary time to get you turned into a Filipino and the details refined.

"Then you mentioned Al. I've sent word to locate him. His headquarters contact thinks he's in the South China Sea. If that is true, we're in luck because it's in character for him to dock in Manila Bay.

"We don't hear from Al very often, with regular reports only once a month. The next report isn't due until seventeen days from now."

Ham smiled as he said, "But we have a ham operator we know trying to raise him. I think we'll have some word by tomorrow."

Lyss smiled too. In the trade this was known as emergency contact.

Before they began their discussion of the method of operation for getting Lyss into Vietnam, Lyss recommended another "old duck" who had served nearly three years in Dalat.

"Last I heard of Jim Shaw," Lyss said, "he was selling real estate in Dallas. He can give us the best information on the town layout. He also knows about the tunnels that were dug there right after Tet."

Ham agreed to get in touch with Jim and to get the latest high resolution pictures from the National

Photographic Interpretation Center.

"If we catch a spot of clear weather, you'll be able to pick out every street and alley of Dalat from the pictures we get now from satellites."

Lyss suggested two alternative plans. First, he thought if properly documented and disguised, he could simply fly into Tan Son Nhut airport at Saigon (Ho Chi Minh City) and take a bus to Dalat.

His second plan was to go into the country illegally by crossing the beach at night north of Nha Trang. He would carry forged documents to protect himself if stopped and questioned.

From the beach, he planned to walk inland and up the mountains to Ban Me Thuot. Lyss felt he could then take a bus to Dalat.

"It has the disadvantage of being slow and will be a physical trial, but I'm in shape for that. I expect to improve my physical condition as a part of my training. What do you think, Ham?"

"You're one of the most brazen bastards I've ever known to think that you could simply take a Filipino passport and walk through Tan Son Nhut Airport, like you did in sixty-seven, and get on a bus and go to Dalat. Frankly, I must admit I think you could do it."

As they continued their discussion, Lyss suggested the landing north of Nha Trang, well north of Cam Ranh Bay, which was now a Soviet base. For the exit, he would bring Harvey to the sea near Hoa Da, a tiny beach hamlet down the mountains about fifty miles from Dalat. Ham agreed with the idea that the devious route through Ban Me Thuot and the more direct exit helped conceal Dalat as the place of operations.

"But how are you going to get him out of prison?"

"My preliminary thought is that if Jim Shaw's tunnel is anywhere close to Harvey's cell, I could dig over to the cell, remove stones from the Bastille wall, and get him out through there. There is much more to think about."

Ham and Lyss rose to their feet, pacing about a bit as they talked. Ham spoke first.

"Sarah will take care of the administrative details, working them out to your satisfaction. Obviously, since you want Al in the act, you have your own ideas about communications. Josh will be available for the gadgetry. We'll see if we can get Jim Shaw.

"Now, as to the immediate problem. I suggest we arrange the accident for tomorrow. How does that fit with your thoughts?"

"Okay," Lyss said. "I think we can do it. I'm having dinner with my son and his family tonight. I can announce my intention to return home tomorrow.

"How about a rendezvous in a highway rest area that has not been opened to the public yet on Interstate 66 between Front Royal and Strasburg?

Pick me up in a chopper. Your security man can take my car on to the mountains west of Staunton where it will be easy for a fast driver to lose control and drop off several hundred feet.

"I'd like for the chopper to take me to a two o'clock rendezvous with Connie. Then we can go on to your country estate."

"Fine. Our place is about thirty minutes by chopper from your farm."

They chatted for a while longer. Sarah fixed some aromatic hot tea. They wandered completely off the current subject and began remembering other things from the past before Vietnam.

Almost frantically, Ham looked at his watch and jumped to his feet.

"I'm on my way. I'll see you at least once more before you set sail, maybe more than once if I can get down there. Good luck, Lyss."

Sarah and Lyss dallied over the tea, then she took him to the club where he had a few minutes of rest before the onslaught of the grandchildren.

He took this opportunity to call Connie. When she answered the phone, he said, "You recognize the voice. Do not use any names. Look for a chopper about two o'clock tomorrow."

She said, "Naturally."

He arrived at his son's home. He hardly had the car door open before his two grandchildren, Linda and

Wesley, rushed out of the house, screaming a welcome. They climbed up his body like squirrels up a tree. There were many hugs and kisses as his daughter-in-law, Cheryl, came out on the porch and ordered the children back into the house.

"Heavens," she said, "I thought they might eat you up." Dinner was roast beef, mashed potatoes, broccoli and a green salad, followed by coffee and an excellent peach cobbler.

"We thought we would splurge a little tonight, Dad," Bobby Lee said. "The pet shop has been doing real well."

"Mighty fine dinner, Cheryl," Lyss said. "I surely appreciate it."

"Granddaddy, I have a new tricycle," Wesley said.

"And I have a Cabbage Patch doll," Linda said.

At no time did the conversation dwell on why Lyss was in Washington. He suspected they were restraining their curiosity. Through the years when he was departing for some faraway place, he would tell Mattie and the children he had a dragon to slay. It was that sharp little Linda, who whispered it gently as she kissed him good night.

"Granddaddy, you go slay that dragon."

Friday morning Lyss took his time, watching parts of the morning television shows. He switched to radio and listened briefly to those two nuts on WMAL, Hardin and Weaver. Then he packed the small bag and checked out of the club.

In a deep and thoughtful mood, Lyss took the downtown route. He circled the great capitol building and marveled again at each of the adjacent buildings and all they stood for. Each building passed brought thoughts to mind of those who had gone on before, some to battle to preserve this great country. He wondered if he would ever see these sights again. He knew the odds were against him. He trembled a bit. As he had told Bobby Lee when he was a boy, a brave man trembled, but went ahead with the job.

With a touch of pride, he thought if he succeeded, he might well be one who had performed a special task to help preserve a free America.

He drove by the Washington obelisk, then across to the Jefferson Monument and back to circle the Lincoln Monument, pausing to look up at that great, kind face.

Through the years he had come in and out of Washington many times. He always came to this monument to pay silent homage to one of his great heroes.

"Abe," he said as he looked up at that massive seated statue, "make room on your lap for my grandkids and smile down on them as they pass by, whether I come by again or not."

As he looked up at that kindly face, he could have sworn Abe winked at him.

The melancholy mood seemed a natural let-

2

down from the past two days, but Lyss knew he would rise above it in a few hours.   He headed west, taking his time.   He arrived at his favorite Front Royal restaurant for early lunch.

The professional in him again began to take hold. He watched the time. The rendezvous was at one o'clock out on Interstate 66. As he pulled into the rest area, weaving around roadblocking barrels and a closed sign, he heard the flapping of the chopper's rotors. He noticed a dark car in the rearview mirror. He had hardly stopped before the chopper settled down.   The dark car stopped.   Sarah stepped out.   Two men brought out a white bedsack from the chopper, obviously heavy with a body.

"Colonel," one of the men said, "step into the chopper and change clothes. Leave everything in your pockets. What little you will need is in the pockets of your new clothes."

He changed. In only a few minutes his clothes had been placed on the body and the body into his car. The young security man took off with Lyss's car, followed by Sarah in the big dark car. She waved a farewell.

Lyss climbed into the chopper, taking the copilot's seat. The chopper slowly rose and then sped west.

The golden yellow of forsythia had touched the Shenandoah valley. The dogwood and redbud still showed their splendor.   In the higher mountains, as they turned southwest, the trees were still barren. Here and there the forest floor gleamed brown and clean, awaiting the new birth of spring. They headed toward Spruce Knob. Lyss thought spring was a good time to start new things.

He shook off his reminiscences as the chopper came close to See's Knob and his West Virginia farm.

Lyss began to navigate for the pilot. Soon they saw the glistening little white farmhouse. Seeing the H of the pad, Lyss ordered the pilot to land.

The rotors were slowly turning, still patting the air, as Lyss saw his small collie come dashing down by the pond, bouncing all over the path. She jumped onto Lyss, nearly knocking him over. He grabbed her collar and restrained her. "Dumb bitch," he said. "I never have been able to train you, and I doubt if anybody could."

He had always complained that his watchdog was silent when someone approached the house, then barked as they left.

"Hell of a watchdog."

Lyss had had a dog as a boy, much smarter than this collie, and had often said he was raised by a dog.

When he had moved to the farm, he wanted a good dog, but instead he got Mitzi. She was a comfort when she quieted down.

Then Lyss saw Connie striding under the great oak toward the pond. He walked swiftly to her.

Because of Lyss's call the previous afternoon,

Connie had been expecting him. They met, embraced, then walked hand in hand up the small slope to the house.

"I have only a few minutes," Lyss said. "Let's sit on the porch."

How many times in nearly forty years had Lyss come home to tell her mother he was off to some far corner? He thought of the night he had left Brooklyn to take the ferry to Staten Island. The troopship convoy waited to take him to Africa and World War II. It was the first time he left his family. It was still vivid in his mind and heart.

Most of his absences had been of short duration. Mattie often accompanied him overseas to live when it was permitted.

"Well, honey, I'm off again."

He spoke rather matter of factly. Connie smiled.

"So what else is new? I knew that was coming up when Ham called the other evening. Where to now, or can you tell me?"

"It's just as well you don't know, but this is a real tough one and will involve a complicated arrangement. I have arranged for you to be briefed. You will be the only family member who will know the facts. I'm hoping you are willing to accept this burden."

He looked at his watch.

"In about an hour or so from now my beautiful little GT will be driven over the edge of Highway 250.

Sometime later you will get a call that I died in it. You must act naturally and go right on with the funeral. You must not tell a single soul, not even Bobby Lee, that you know better. One of Ham's boys will get in touch with you soon. Meanwhile, handle it just as though my death were real, the cremation, the funeral service, and later, the insurance and taxes. Only you will know it wasn't my body that was cremated. I know it will be hard on Bobby Lee and the kids and on you."

He embraced her again and kissed her cheek where now one tear glistened. He kissed it away and held her briefly in his arms.

"Daddy," she said with emotion, "I'm terribly proud our country would ask you to do such a service. As hard as it will be, I'll do my part."

"It's wonderful to have a daughter like you," Lyss said.

"When I come back, if I come back, we'll develop an explanation. Let's worry about that when the time comes. The assignment is a personal one from the President.

"I had dinner with Bobby Lee, Cheryl, and the kids last night. They send their love.

"Anyway, I'm on my way. If I'm lucky, I'll be back in six months or so, maybe less. If I'm not lucky, the President will tell you and Bobby Lee personally."

He embraced her again, then broke away and went to the helicopter.

DRAGONS YET TO SLAY

CHAPTER SIX

The seat belt was barely buckled before the rotor blades began their pistol-shot cracks and the chopper lifted off, tilted and swiftly headed east, then southeast. Massive Cheat Mountain passed underneath, complete with its hardwood cover and patches of dense laurel so typical of the mountains of West Virginia.

In the higher elevations the pine trees dominated. Early harvesting had left most of them as young, brilliantly green and lovely in the winter snow.

Lyss wondered if he would ever see it again, or like the bear Clayton Walker had shot, would his flesh and bones slowly disintegrate in some undiscovered spot in the woods?

He began to wonder about the destination of the helicopter. It would be new to him, whose original clandestine instruction had been given in a Tidelands location. The chopper came down near the mountaintops. Lyss saw the Blue Ridge in the eastern distance. Below him was the Shenandoah River, the beautiful valley where Lyss's ancestors had farmed before the American Revolution.

The chopper began its descent. The pilot turned out over the river, then back toward the west with the green Appalachian foothills blossoming with the first touch of spring.

They settled down in the vast expanse of grounds in front of an ancient, red brick, Georgian style mansion. Not another house was in sight in any direction. They were isolated, as Lyss expected them to be.

He dismounted from the chopper and started walking toward the portico. He was only a few steps away when the chopper took off. Lyss was alone in the front yard. He felt a bit eerie, with no luggage, no identification and in a strange place.

Before he reached the first steps, the front door opened and a black man emerged, dressed in a light seersucker suit, white shirt and black bow tie.

My God, Lyss thought. *They've brought me to Tara.* This black man, complete with bow tie, was a perfect character for *Gone With the Wind*.

"Welcome to Green Acres, Mr. Moorman."

During his stay at the place, he was to be Upton Moorman.   During his entire sojourn at the mansion, not a single person was supposed to call him by any other name, even those who knew him well.

"My name is Charles, sir. I'm here to serve you in every way I can. May I show you your room?"

Lyss nodded. They entered the center hall which was dominated by a great crystal chandelier hanging from the second floor ceiling. Circular stairways went up on the left and on the right. The center hall had two small groups on either side, a table, a lamp and two chairs on either side.

They took the stairs to the second floor where a railing overlooked the first floor of the center hall.

They turned left. Lyss was shown into a spacious sitting room with doors on both left and right walls. Charles showed him into the bedroom at the left.

"Cocktails are at six o'clock, sir," Charles said. "Dinner is usually at seven-thirty if that pleases you."

Lyss nodded. Charles left the room.

Lyss began an exploration, first the bathroom where he found the cabinet filled with necessities. There was his type of Schick razor, Gillette foamy lather, Mennen Afta Shave and Vitalis hair tonic. There was even a bottle of Ecotrin, coated aspirin tablets. The medicine cabinet, on the wall over the lavatory, had a mirror for a door. He looked at himself and wondered what the face in the mirror would look like in a few weeks.

In the bedroom, he opened the dresser drawer to find shirts, socks, shorts, and handkerchiefs. The closet had three suits, three pairs of shoes and three one piece jumpsuits. In the corner of the huge closet was a bag with a tennis racquet. He opened it to find blazing yellow shorts, a Chevy Chase Country Club tennis shirt, balls and visor.

"I don't think they have forgotten a thing," Lyss said.

He stripped, stepped into the shower and luxuriated in the steamy water for a few minutes, then dried off and tried on some of the new clothes. The shorts were white cotton. Then he picked out a blue dress shirt, which he left open at the collar and a pair of navy blue trousers of worsted material. There was a black leather belt. All of the clothing was his size. Every piece had the label removed.

When he had finished dressing, he found a Seiko watch on the dresser and put it on.

It was five thirty. Lyss thought this eventful day had passed mighty quickly.

He returned to the sitting room to find several pieces of Louis XVI tables and chairs, with lamps of silver and glass. The couch was covered in biege fabric. In front of a nineteen inch television was a huge reclining rocker, also covered with biege fabric.

On the walls were three large oil paintings, one a copy of Gainsborough's *Blue Boy*, two of rural autumn scenes.

He found a shelf of books and picked at random.

He found Halberstam's *The Best and the Brightest*. A stereo system stood against one wall with a small library of cassettes.   He picked out Eugene Ormandy and the Philadelphia Symphony Orchestra playing *Scheherazade*.

During one of the more somber passages, Lyss set down the book and walked to the window. The music put him in a blue mood, wondering if his facial surgery would be painful after the anesthetic wore off. He put his hand on his face and trembled a bit. He was frightened, but he shook it off.

He began to walk around. Idly he looked into the room opposite his bedroom and found a matching bedroom. Exploring the hall, he realized this home was really huge. There were eleven doors off the straight hall with the open area of the entry hall taking up the space of what would have been another room.

The doors were locked, he presumed, and tried one, which confirmed his guess.

He returned to the sitting room of his suite and looked out the large window, which was really twin glass doors opening onto a small balcony. He stepped out and breathed beautiful air and looked into the side of the mountain, the eastern portion of his beloved Appalachians.

Closer to the house was a concrete tennis court enclosed in a high fence. Off to the right were a garage and a rather large red barn.

No southern estate was complete without either a red barn or a huge white one. Lyss saw evidence of a full swimming pool on the south side of the house.

"I'm sure, somewhere there's at least a putting green."

A glance at his watch showed it was just past six, so he turned off the stereo and went down the stairs. In the area under his room, but stretching from the front to the back of the building, was a large living room. It was exquisitely furnished. In one corner there was a small grouping of chairs with a television. He moved over to the TV and turned it on. After a bit of searching he found the CBS national news. The world was in its usual mess.

Charles had brought him a bowl of ice, a bottle of Chivas Regal and a pitcher of water. Lyss poured scotch over ice in a glass and added a splash of water. As he sipped he thought soon he must hold his drinking and eating habits to conform with his new identity.

"Oh well, I'll enjoy this while I can."

As he sat in the comfortable reclining chair in front of the television, he was surprised that the CBS station he had found was a Washington station. The local news had been going only a few minutes before the announcement of his accident came.

"This has just been handed to me. Colonel Ulysses McCutcheon, formerly of Washington and a veteran of three wars, was killed this afternoon in a one car accident on Highway 250 west of Staunton. State police say the car was apparently traveling at a high rate of speed, failed to make one of the curves and plunged off a steep incline into Germany Valley.

We have no further details at this time, but it is likely such a highly decorated soldier as Colonel McCutcheon will be buried with full honors in Arlington National Cemetery."

Lyss got up and prepared a second drink. How peculiar to hear his own obituary. There were two times in his life in which the doctors thought he would die. The first was from wounds he had received at Kasserine Pass in World War II when three shell fragments had ripped into his abdomen. He had been bandaged up, and an IV of glucose had been inserted in a vein. At least they told him that was what happened. He was unconscious, primarily from loss of blood.

In the General Hospital in Algiers they had worked feverishly over his carcass, giving him blood transfusions as they cut into him to patch up torn intestines.

Two months had passed before he had been permitted to return to the Third Division. By this time his outfit had landed behind the expanding beachhead at Salerno in Italy. The 3rd had entered the line and had reached the Volturno River.

Lyss had returned to his company before it assaulted across the river. He was rewarded for his actions in that battle with the Distinguished Service Cross. He had already received the Silver Star for his work in the landing in Morocco. He was later to receive another DSC, although his division commander, General Kevin O'Keefe, had recommended him for the Medal of Honor for aggressively leading a patrol in the Colmar Pocket in France right after Christmas of 1944.

He had been lucky and brash as a young man. He preferred in his later years such nice things as the Legion of Merit General Chandler Boone gave him in Vietnam. Being under enemy fire was not a qualification for the Legion of Merit.

Then his mind wandered to his second waltz with death, which had been only two years ago. He awoke at one thirty one October morning with blood pouring from his nose. He went to the bathroom, poured cold water on the back of his neck, put cotton in his nose, but the blood poured back into his throat. He woke Mattie. She called the ambulance. They took him to Memorial Hospital in Elkins.

The ambulance was manned by three of his best Valley Head friends. One of these friends was riding in the back with Lyss's head in his lap. The bleeding had stopped, but Lyss was dizzy.

"I guess," he said, "if you've got to die, it's best to die in the arms of a dear friend."

He had lost about five pints of blood and his blood pressure was seventy, not seventy over something, just seventy.

When he had recovered, he went to Walter Reed Army Medical Center in Washington, where they issued him a Noz-Stop, a peculiar little rubber gadget with an inflatable bulb on each end. He was taught its proper use. It blocked the bleeding and within a few hours could be removed.

Lyss realized he must have a Noz-Stop, which he had nicknamed Excalibur, to take with him on his mission. How could he get it without alerting the doctors to his problem? They might consider it disabling and not permit him to continue.

Then his thoughts centered on the news he had just received from the television. The young security officer and Sarah had accomplished their mission in a highly successful manner.

Some tears came to his eyes as he thought of the heartache he knew was felt in his son's home. He imagined young Wesley would be asking his parents what it meant that Granddaddy was dead. Lyss wondered if the mission was worth it. The cost of patriotism was sometimes high and often spread over several generations. He had said his love of his country was one of the main reasons why he was undertaking this dangerous task, but the penalties were being paid by his children, his grandchildren and his friends.

DRAGONS YET TO SLAY

CHAPTER SEVEN

His reverie was broken up by the entrance of a man and a woman. The man immediately put out his hand in greeting.

"I'm Dr. Stravinsky, but my friends find it easier to call me Dr. Tom. This is Nurse Williams. We're here as a part of this clambake."

Lyss had known he would be subjected to a close physical examination as a part of this job. He had always approached physical exams with some anxiety.

He was worried they might find something disqualifying, like cancer or the nosebleeds. In the past, his fears of such encounter always came to nothing. He had easily passed every physical he had taken in his many years of service. He put up with the humorous chiding of some doctors, who complained that after passing the age of fifty his waist had increased from thirty inches to a massive thirty-four.

"A little bit of potbelly adds to a man's maturity," he told the doctor. "Although I guess I'd really rather be Johnny Weismuller than Ben Franklin."

"Much of your program here will be entwined with medical procedures," Dr. Tom said. "You will often think we're not only interfering, but managing your life. For example, before you eat dinner tonight, Nurse Williams needs to take some of your hillbilly blood, and after dinner I would like to give you a thorough physical exam. It is my understanding that time is important."

"That's true as I understand it, Doc," Lyss said.

"I will set aside this drink and await your pleasure for taking blood from this fine old turnip."

Nurse Williams took him upstairs where he discovered two fully equipped medical rooms. One of them appeared to be a complete surgery.

When she finished, Lyss joined the doctor, followed by Nurse Williams in fifteen minutes. They all went into the dining room.

The dinner was excellent, Lyss thought. He wondered how much longer he would have such good food. The menu included sauteed shrimp and Alaskan king crab legs. Chocolate mousse and coffee topped the meal.

"Well, let's go take a look at your aging carcass," the doctor said, pushing back his chair and getting to his feet.

Nurse Williams excused herself, saying she was taking the turnip blood into the computer lab where she had made special arrangements for an overnight analysis.

Lyss and the doctor went upstairs to what he learned to call the infirmary. He sat at the side of the doctor's desk. They spent some time reviewing his medical history. Lyss was surprised that, even though he had retired three years ago, the doctor had his file from the medical records of the agency.

It was nearly bedtime when he was dismissed, so he crossed the hall and went into his own rooms. It had been a long, hard day, and he would not have to be rocked to sleep.

After breakfast, Lyss walked around the grounds, and found the barn contained considerable gymnasium equipment, the tennis court had a coating over the concrete and the swimming pool was Olympic size.

As he walked back to the mansion he thought about the fine planning, and efficiency so great it was almost offensive, that had gone into setting up this establishment.

When he got back to the house, he was delighted to see Sarah had arrived and Nurse Williams had returned. They were seated on the east veranda.

Sarah rose and accepted a kiss.

He shook hands with the nurse and nodded toward the doctor.

"I think we can discuss your condition out here," the doctor said as Sarah brought out a notepad.

The doctor complimented him on his physical condition at fifty-eight and said he would approve him for overseas service, which was the standard required for the project.

"I don't think your nosebleed problem is disabling, but you ought to carry a Noz-Stop with you. I'll get you one," the doctor said. "I might add that the scars I detected are well healed and pliable. We are not permitted the luxury of curiosity in the intelligence business. Nevertheless, would you mind telling us how you got that large scar on your abdomen and the gash in your left side?"

Lyss was pleased.

"The only really serious wound I've received in three wars, Doctor Tom, was at Kasserine Pass in World War II. They say three shell fragments hit me in the belly. It took fancy surgery to get the guts patched up. The gash in the left side was courtesy of a Sicilian who took umbrage at some work I had done. He met me, by accident on my part I assure you, in an alley of Sorrento. Fortunately my ribs took most of it, but between the ribs he did manage to nick the left lung. It healed quickly.   The Sicilian did not heal.

"While I'm at it, I may as well tell you the bullet scar in the right shoulder was from the Viet Cong during Tet. It was strictly a flesh wound. Those, Dr. Tom, are all the wounds I got from three wars. I'm incredibly lucky."

"Interesting, Mr. Moorman, very interesting. I thank you for sharing it with us."

"Let's go upstairs for a shot. It's best we get started on the pigmentation process."

Lyss found the morning interesting with physical therapists in the gym moving him from one exercise to another and monitoring his heart in the process. They seemed happy. He showered and wore his Philippine shirt to lunch.

Sarah was there. They picked at the shrimp salad and ice tea before Lyss announced his intention to take a short nap.

"Good night, Upton. Tennis at three o'clock," Sarah said with a bit of a smile on her face.

After his nap and reading a few pages, Lyss took the tennis clothes from the closet. Some joker had put in a pair of size thirty shorts, instead of thirty-four. The other pair were okay. They had even provided his favorite racquet.

Arriving at the tennis court a few minutes before three, Lyss was surprised to find the doctor rallying with the two physical therapists. He was also surprised at the quality of the hitting, all three pounding the ball with sharp cracks of the racquets.

It was obviously good tennis.

"Can you stand a medical partner, Mr. Moorman?"

"Delighted, Doctor. Let's see if these young men can make life interesting."

Then Sarah arrived dressed in a tennis skirt

that exposed shapely legs. She announced she would referee this match and she would not put up with any temper tantrums.

The doctor was an excellent player at the net. Lyss had always been what most tennis players called a good retriever, covering a lot of court. So it was an interesting match. By the end of two sets everyone was wet with sweat from the activity in the spring sunshine.

Gathering up his gear, Lyss turned to find Sarah waiting. She linked her arm in his. They walked to the mansion. She accompanied him to the parlor of his room and announced that, at her request, the other room off that parlor was hers.

He closed the door and took her in his arms.

"There's something amorous about the clean sweat of a healthy man," she said, ardently returning his kiss.

They went into his bedroom.

Later the group was gathered in the TV corner for drinks and a somewhat casual watch of the evening news when a huge man entered the room. Josh Rosenbloom towered over everyone at six feet six and probably weighed 250 pounds.

He grabbed Lyss and lifted him off his feet in a mighty embrace.

"What cha gotcha self into these days?" Josh asked. "What dragon you out to slay?"

"How did a Jew get so damned big?" Lyss said with a broad smile.

"I think maybe instead of having David as an ancestor, Goliath got in there someway."

During the filet mignon dinner, Lyss recalled some of this huge Jew's past. Josh was born in Brooklyn and proud of it. His speech was right out of the streets. Lyss recalled the shock waves that went through him when he learned this great bear, whose grammar had driven a number of English teachers to distraction, had a degree in electrical engineering from Massachusetts Institute of Technology.

Lyss asked Josh and Sarah to join him in his sitting room.

"I'm going into Vietnam illegally, and I need some personal defense materials. What do you recommend?"

"Of course, yer hung up because yer an American, so shootin' first is out and you gotta live after the other feller shoots at you. So why not git the old 9mm Browning, which shoots seven bullets. You can tuck it in yer belt without no more bulge than what God and overeatin' gave you. By the time you git to shoot, you'll have to be damn fast to git off two rounds, so seven is aplenty. I think they got it on the store shelf."

He turned to Sarah. She nodded.

"I'll check into it tomorrow."

"Then," Josh said, "if yer still as nasty at close fightin' as you was, you oughta have a stiletto. They got a good one which has flip-up guards. They gotta new Ace-of-Spades type belt buckle made of glass and plastic, but tough as steel the old Ace-of-Spades was made uv. It don't show on no X-ray machine and fits yer fist."

"You 'member the old stun gun, one shot fountain pen, made to knock a guy out and not kill him? It's .22 caliber and shoots a plastic bullet. Gotta be kinda close for it to knock a guy out.

"And a new gadget that's dirty pool, but I sure like it, is the ballpoint pen that will write, but when handled right is a hypo for shootin' some knockout drops into a guy. The enemy is out in five seconds and stays that way for thirty minutes or so.

"Got some plastic bullets for the 9mm, too, but it ain't easy to be delicate with them and just stun some unlucky bastard what gets in yer way. Natch, we got reglar bullets if you want to kill some character and get yer ass before a shootin' hearing."

"Jesus!" Lyss laughed.

"Now how about some miniature communications?"

"Well, they done a good job fixin' up the old cigarette pack. It can transmit, receive and record squirt. That squirt is somethin' else. It transmits a twenty second message in two seconds."

"That sounds good to me," Lyss said. "We'll also need the base units to put aboard a ship."

"Josh and I will go in and raid the storeroom tomorrow," Sarah said.   "If he's available, we'll return here in the afternoon. Josh can brief you on each item. We'll have to take them back and pouch them to Manila."

"Now, you spies, I suggest brandy and coffee on the veranda."

Dragons Yet To Slay

CHAPTER EIGHT

Time seemed to pass by swiftly, Lyss thought, but at other times it seemed to take so long to get routine things done.

Each day developed into a set routime. A certain time was always devoted to physical conditioning, a long time each day to language training and few moments with the doctor as he worked diligently to change the physical appearance. Lyss's complexion was swarthy, almost brown. His nose was spread at the nostrils.

"I'm fairly good lookin', for a Filipino," Lyss said.

All his life Lyss had been careful to keep his muscle tone and to keep his weight within reason. So he was somewhat surprised when the physical regimen caused him to lose several pounds.

"It still didn't firm up my little potbelly," he said to Dr. Tom.

Unlike most men of medium stature, Lyss was not a speedster on the track. He was well known for his stamina and endurance in the longer runs. Sometimes he had some difficulty with long hikes over rough terrain.

Lyss set himself up to work on climbing both slopes and mountains. Two or three times a week he took to the steep slopes of the Appalachians guarding the west side of the estate.

Lyss deliberately sought out vertical cliffs and steep slopes. He felt they would be better training for possible climbs in Vietnam. He carried pitons with him and a long coil of rope. This enabled him to go up some cliffs in his lone operation. Sometimes he tried a mountain face that was too difficult for him. It discouraged him.

On those occasions when she spent the day at the mansion, Sarah would accompany him on a climb. He was amazed at her strength and agility. She would leap from rock to rock like some mountain goat. Sometimes her enthusiastic approach turned out to be more than she could do, and she would have to stop and rest.

It was an incident of his mountain climbing that brought on a big argument between Lyss and Sarah. Lyss had enjoyed taking her with him on climbs that could be made by a solitary climber, so he decided to go one better and take on a cliff face that would require two climbers.

"No way, Buster," Sarah had said with anger in her voice. "It's stupid for you to want to try a two-man climb. You have no need for it, since you will be a singleton in Vietnam. I think you are just on an ego trip. I won't have any part of it."

She left the mansion that afternoon, earlier than originally scheduled. She did not return for nearly a week.

When she did come back, she took Lyss aside. They compromised. Lyss agreed to just the one joint climb. "After that, I'll be a good boy," he said.

"But I still want to know why you want to climb that cliff," Sarah said.

"It's a challenge, my dear," he said. "It seems to me if I tackle a tougher task, it'll make lesser ones seem easier than they are. I know I can't do this one alone. Maybe I can't do it even with your help, but I want to try."

"Besides, you know why men climb mountains, because they're there," he said with a wide grin.

So they attacked the almost vertical face, with occasional insets that multiplied the problems.

The early part of the climb was not difficult. Then they reached a place where the cliff overhang made an outward reach necessary.

Lyss carefully placed the pitons closer as they were located almost over his head. Twice as he tested a spike, it pulled loose. Seeking better and more secure places, he became absorbed in the cliff. He was about twelve feet ahead of Sarah, just above one of the insets, when the top piton gave way and Lyss plunged down, swung on the holding spike and slammed into the rock face.

Sarah quickly secured the rope around a small tree growing out of the lower face, keeping him from falling further.

She called to Lyss but got no answer, so she hurried to him, then back to the rope and gently let him down to the easier slope. He was unconscious.

She unlatched the rope and harness and laid him carefully on the slope. Blood oozed from a bruise on the left side of his head. She bathed it with water from her canteen.

She could not decide whether she should go back to the mansion and get help or stay with Lyss. She decided to stay, bathing his face and the bruised spot. Finally, she was relieved as his eyes fluttered. Then he opened his eyes.

He hung his head a bit and grinned.

"I guess I can't climb this mountain, at least not here. I hope that knocked some sense into my feeble brain."

Then he rose and they walked back to the mansion with Sarah keeping a watchful eye.

Nurse Williams was there and bathed the head bruise, suggesting it would be better to leave it exposed to the air. She found cuts on the right hand, cleaned and bandaged them.

It was during this process that Lyss began to realize the lesson learned. There were things he could not do. He was mortal.

It was not until they went out on the veranda and Charles brought them drinks, that Lyss turned to Sarah, feeling love and gratitude.

"You're wonderful."

His voice choked. That was all he could say.

Then he realized how much he had looked forward to her visits, which came only once or twice a week.

It dawned on him that such a fight as they had had the previous week might cause her to abandon him, except as a professional. He knew her pride in the outfit was too great to permit anything like that to cause her to ask to be relieved as the case officer.

When the thought crossed Lyss's mind that she might abandon him, he realized he had a deep, abiding love for her. He recognized nothing could be done until the mission was completed. He felt that she loved him, too. It was the first time he thought of marrying her when the job was done.

Despite the bruises and cuts, he felt remarkably well. Even so, he was amazed at what he saw in the mirror. His skin had turned a light coffee color. The gray had left his hair. Minor surgery had modified his nose by widening the base and extending the nostrils.

"Not bad," he said to himself, "but by God I hope they can restore my Scotch-Irish face when this is over."

"I don't think anybody, even looking hard, could tell me from a real Filipino," he told Sarah one night over supper.

Sarah was having her own problem adjusting to the change in physical appearance. She also hoped that he would be restored to the same old hillbilly she loved when he returned.

"I love you for what you are inside, not your nose and brown skin," she said to Lyss.

His hardest labor came with the intensive language study. He spent hours in the little recording booth with earphones on, listening to one of two languages he was attempting to perfect, Vietnamese and Tagalog, with emphasis on the Vietnamese.

Tagalog, the second largest ethnic language group in the Philippines, had blended a great deal of the islands ethnic history: Chinese, Malay, Hindu, Japanese, Spanish and Portugese. English and Spanish had been used for years. Most of the great leaders of the Philippines had come from the ranks of the Tagalogs.

"You can always fake a Tagalog accent," Lyss said.

It was Tagalog that was giving him the most difficulty. The Vietnamese came slowly. It was good Vietnamese he needed most. His French came back easily, but he realized as a Filipino, he would have damned little use for French.

One evening each week a native speaker of one or the other would show up. Their entire conversation would be in the language of the native.

So he was almost exhuberant when, at last, Tran thi Nguyen complimented him on his clarity of speech in Vietnamese and his affected Tagalog accent.

He was in a third set of singles with one of the physical therapists when Hamilton Campbell strolled out to the court, followed by a short, swarthy man whom Lyss instantly recognized.

He dropped his racquet and dashed over to grab Jim Shaw and give him a hug.

"Do I know you, you character?" Jim smiled. "Where's that patrician nose and genuine American tan? By God, they sure have done a hell of a job on you."

"You know darned good and well where they've gone," Lyss replied. "Let me finish off this upstart. I'll be right with you."

The friendship of Jim Shaw and Lyss went back fifteen years, when they were in Honolulu on the staff of the Commander in Chief, Pacific. Jim was a lieutenant colonel, U.S. Air Force, and Lyss was in uniform of an Army colonel, but both of them were working for the CIA.

From Jim's deep tanned complexion, Lyss knew he was continuing his addiction for golf. They had played golf together twice a week for two years. Jim was good at it.

Jim's wife Eva and Lyss's Mattie had been close friends, too, during those two glorious Hawaiian years.

A graduate of the A. and M. College of Texas, Jim had served in three wars, but had gone into the real estate business in Dallas when he retired.

"Real estate doesn't interfere with my golf," he said, "like a regular job of some kind would."

He was a handsome man, balding somewhat, with an infectious chuckle that made him almost instantly liked, even by strangers.

He had served in Dalat as chief province adviser during the time Lyss was in Saigon. When Jim had to come to Saigon he stayed with Lyss. He never voluntarily left Dalat, whose nine hole golf course pleased him more than the eighteen hole course in Saigon.

"Besides," he once said, "those damned incoming rockets have shorely made a thirty-six hole course out of Saigon's eighteen holer."

Upon learning they would spend the night, Lyss relaxed and went up for his shower. Ham and Jim set up an easel in the parlor area, displaying a magnified version of an aerial photo of Dalat.

"The Boss and I have been chinning on the way down," Jim said.

"I agree Harvey is probably in that big hunk of gray stone we called the Bastille.

"I figured he's in one of the cells across the north side of the basement. We got in there every once in a while to try to get the ARVN to stop the torturing and use simpler interrogation methods. We tried to explain that what a man said after he quit screaming from burns and electric shock was not accurate.

"We never used intelligence from such interrogations unless we could check it out with another source.

"Here is a recon photo taken from a satellite just six days ago. Man, look how clear and sharp that picture is. We're mighty lucky that satellite caught a day of sunshine and no clouds. Cloudless days were scarce in Dalat.

"You can see the Bastille on the east edge of the mountain, and the outer wall goes around the entire compound."

Jim was using a pointer like a briefing officer.

"This is the house we used for principal headquarters. It's about a hundred yards from the northwest edge of the compound. It's two hundred and fifty yards from the edge of the mountain."

He turned to both Ham and Lyss with a wide grin.

"I know because we tunneled it. I measured it carefully and included it in my report.

"Now the tunnel goes about here, passing within ten feet of the north wall. The east entrance of the tunnel comes out in the side of the mountain. We blocked it up with stone, which could be easily removed in case we had to hurry out that way. The tunnel came to mind after that three-day siege we had during Tet.

"The Boss says you think you might dig a tunnel from our old tunnel, if it's still there, into the basement of the Bastille. There were spots of tough digging. The wall itself might give you trouble, but I think you could do it.

"The first thing you must do is get possession of our old headquarters house. I think money would talk, particularly gold.

"We rented from a nephew of Nguyen Cao Ky, before he became premier of South Vietnam, while he was still in the Vietnamese Air Force. I always suspected that flashy character owned it himself as a rental property, or his wife did. In any case, we were charged very little rent.

"That guy Ky was one of my favorites. He was the president before Nguyen Van Thieu. I thought he did a better job of running the country. He wasn't the politician Thieu was.

"You may have trouble finding who owns it today, but, again, gold does a lot of talking. If Vo Van Son is still there, and I suspect he is, you could find out from him. Watch out for that dog. He's treacherous.

"Now your next big job is to find which cell Harvey is in. That won't be easy, friend. I'm sure you'll figure a way. Here's a sketch I made from memory of those cells across the north side. They're rather big for prison cells, three meters wide by three meters deep. That's close to ten feet square. My memory is that there are six of them."

Jim paused and reached over to a Coke on the nearby table.

"The same source who told us Harvey was in Dalat, also told us there were three other prisoners in that building," Ham said.

"Two were Vietnamese, who apparently had not accepted the reindoctrination their captors had decided was important. Why they were not sent into the rice fields to work on a change of mind and heart is a mystery.

"The third prisoner was a Filipino. I am checking him out. He apparently was a former employee of Occidental Construction, who helped us build the Cam Ranh Bay facilities.

"If he is still there, he might be the excuse for you to get into the building and get a good look at it all.

"I am not going to tell you how to do it, or even if you are to do it. You will be there, and the tough decisions are yours to make.

"His name is Jose Mendoza. He is about forty years old."

He went on to report that the weapons, considerable gold coin and the communications equipment had been sent by pouch to the Manila Station.

Ham told Lyss he was due out the next day, going to Manila via Taipei. He was to be met by a Filipino agent, whose sign would be an invitation to Baguio. Lyss's countersign was to be "It's too wet this time of year."

He reported that the *Pharaon* had docked in Manila that day, and Al was eager about the project.

Sarah arrived. The men started to get up.

"Keep your seats, gentlemen," Sarah said. "We have a small bit of business. Senor Juan Farrar, here is your passport."

It was the first time Lyss had heard the name he would be using. He took the Filipino passport and tucked it into one of the voluminous shirt pockets.

"And, Senor, your wallet and two packets of money. There are five hundred dollars in U.S. currency, common in the Philippines, and the equivalent of one thousand dollars in Vietnamese currency. Your gold is being pouched to Manila. Most Filipinos carry a lucky peso. One is tucked into your wallet. Your identification, driver's license, membership in a Manila club, are all legitimate. All will be honored in Manila, even the private club. I don't think you will have much time to use it.

"Okay, guys, feed this starving girl."

They proceeded downstairs and to the usual cocktail corner. With a wide grin on his face, Charles brought out a tray of San Miguel beer.

"Not tonight, Charles," Lyss said. "I want one last fling at the niceties of my true ancestors. Chivas Regal, please."

"Wait a minute, Charles," Hamilton said. "Bring us that special bottle I brought with me."

Soon, a tall bottle of twenty-five year old Glenmorangie was brought out. Even those who normally did not drink scotch yielded to the selection.

They all filled their glasses, and Ham lifted his. "Success."

Sarah lifted her glass.

"And long life!"

They all stood and faced Lyss. Every eye was moist. Glasses clinked as they understood the double meaning of Sarah's toast. Lyss wondered if he would ever be back with this group.

The table quieted down as they savored the good food and a bottle of Pedroncelli's Cabernet Sauvignon.

At last Ham rose.

"Lyss, and I am consciously violating security by using your name, I will report to the Director tomorrow that you are launched. Jim and I will return to Washington tonight. Sarah will remain and will take you to the airport tomorrow.

"She and Josh will head for Manila a day after you. They will definitely see you before the *Pharaon* sets sail. So if you have any last minute thoughts, you will be able to pass them on. Josh will check out all the communications equipment.

"Our prayers go with you."

They left.

Sarah took one last sip of the lovely wine, then she rose. Lyss followed her upstairs.

In the privacy of the joint parlor, she reached up to wrap her arms around his neck. He kissed her eagerly.

An hour later, they lay exhausted in each other's arms.

"This, my love, must last a long time," Sarah said.

"Yes, Sarah darling, yes."

CHAPTER NINE

The sea was blue-green seven miles below, the solid white of the cloud cover having given way shortly after leaving Honolulu. Lyss was in a window seat, forward of the wing. Was this to be his last flight over this tremendous ocean? His first flight across the Pacific had been eastbound from Tokyo in 1958.

In those days, if the flight was of long duration, the government provided first class accommodations. Lyss was not only given first class, but a bunk in a DC-7, then the biggest plane in the air. He had given the bunk to a young mother and her baby.

Then he recalled his first ocean flight, in a DC-4, which the Army Air Corps called a C-54, leaving from Frankfurt in June, 1945, stopping at Prestwick in Scotland, at Halifax in Nova Scotia, then New York's old La Guardia. It took two days in bucket seats on the military transport. Many of the passengers had simply stretched out on the floor for sleep.

Lyss remembered the fine railroad travel right after World War II when Pullman cars were upgraded and the railroads still prided themselves in fine service, including magnificent dining facilities. It made the three day, coast to coast trip a real pleasure.

Today Lyss would have five meals. His first was breakfast at the mansion, then breakfast over the Rockies en route from Washington to Los Angeles, lunch en route to Honolulu, and before arrival in Taipei Lyss had lunch again. If all went well in Taipei, Lyss would have dinner that night in Manila.

Lyss, seasoned traveler that he was, ate sparingly of each offering. He was dreaming a bit as he toyed with the lunch when he suddenly realized the pretty little stewardess was speaking to him in Tagalog.

"Regrets," he said in Tagalog, hoping his accent was accepted. "What was it you said?"

"I just asked if you would care for a bit more wine," she replied. "I don't get to see many of my countrymen on this run, but I guess Americans are my countrymen now since I have my citizenship."

"Where were you born?"

"Luzon, north of Manila, in San Jose."

"I know it well," Lyss said. "Some of the best northern bananas are grown there."

She had to leave because of her duties. Lyss was relieved his accent apparently had not raised any question.

The incident brought to mind some of the

history of the Philippines, especially in the past two centuries when Spanish influence was heavy until replaced by the Americans after the Spanish-American War.

His thoughtful mood brought him to recalling the motor trip from the mansion to Dulles Airport. Sarah had bid him farewell as he boarded one of those buses built on stilts to leave the airport building for the airplane.

The flight to Los Angeles had been uneventful. He had looked down on some storms over the Mississippi valley, then clear skies over the Rockies. While he was partial to his native Appalachians, Lyss loved the grandeur and the massivesness of the Rockies, especially in Colorado over which they had flown. Los Angeles was the usual mass of people, all going different directions.

Lyss had always disliked the massive, smog ridden metropolis which was Los Angeles, avoiding it whenever possible. It was a bit tough, he once said, to leave the clear, crisp air of West Virginia and get to LA and breath that crap.

He had enjoyed looking from the secure area of the Honolulu airport across to see that Diamond Head was still a sentinel of Hawaii, even though somewhat overshadowed by the massive man made towers one group in Hawaii and tried for years to prevent.

Now it was still technically midday as they winged over the Pacific. He was always in awe of the great spaciousness of the northern Pacific. The northern distances were dwarfed by the vast expanses of the South Pacific.

Things went well in the beautiful, clean Taipei airport. He took his carry-on luggage into the men's room and changed from his dark gray suitcoat and white shirt to a Philippine shirt, the famous barong Tagalog, complete with ruby cuff links. His dress for arrival in Manila had been specified by Sarah.

As he cleared customs and immigration in Manila, Lyss saw a swarthy, smiling man, only slightly larger than himself. "Would you like to visit Baguio, sir?" the man said.

As directed by Ham, Lyss said, "It is too wet this time of year."

The man waved a hand and a *jeepney* taxi roared up, burning some rubber as it screeched to a halt.

The *jeepney* with all its gaudy painting was a product of post World War II and the ingenuity of the Filipino drivers. They took American military jeeps and put a roof and seats in the back, then decorated it all lavishly with red, yellow, gold, and enough blue to offset the brighter colors. Most had scrolls of gold down the sides.

Lyss's luggage was loaded aboard and they took off. Took off was a good description, thought Lyss, because the *jeepney* driver obviously believed speed and maneuvering for advantage were the keys to his success.

They headed into town and passed the Manila Hotel. Lyss noted a tower had been added to the rear wing, but the famous MacArthur suite was still evident at the penthouse level of the old portion.

It was in this suite that the imperious Douglas MacArthur lived while training the Philippine Army in its early days. Then he had returned, as promised, in the fading days of World War II. He became the symbol of resurrected freedom and the proponent of a new independence.

It was no coincidence that the day chosen for the beginning of the Republic of the Philippines was the Fourth of July, 1946.

In the hustle and bustle of the old town, the *jeepney* and its occupants wove their way to what appeared to be an ancient apartment building, the dirt, the carbon and the dust of centuries evident.

They piled out. Two young Filipinos came from the door to grab the bags and take them inside.

The third floor apartment they entered was remarkably clean. It was also small as were most apartments of their vintage, which Lyss guessed to be about 1950. Most of Manila was built after the war.

His companion held a finger to his lips and pointed to the walls and light fixtures. Thus Lyss knew the place had not been swept for bugs and other devices.

"It is good to have you home, Senor Farrar," his companion said, handing him a card with the name

Julio on it.

"Good to see you again, Julio."

"I have arranged that you will go north to Lingayen Gulf either tomorrow or next day by boat, a small yacht that is available."

"That's good. What time is it now?"

"It is five after six."

Lyss took off the Seiko watch and punched the time and new date into the proper place.

"I'm not going to bed very early," Lyss said. "Although I've been up for more than twenty-four hours, a few more won't hurt me. Is there a place near here where we can get a light supper?"

"Not too near, but an American friend has invited me to dinner and asked me to bring you along."

Shades of old Saigon days, thought Lyss. There would be a bit of conversation tonight.

"Well, let me clean up. When you say so, we'll go meet with your friend."

They went out the back way, not for security reasons, Lyss learned, but because that was where the slightly beat up Ford sedan was kept. They drove back west, passing the Manila Hotel again, going down a beautiful wide boulevard. Lyss recalled it was called Dewey Boulevard, after the famous American commodore, in the days when the Philippines was a commonwealth of the USA. It was not renamed for some fifteen years after independence was granted in 1946.

They passed the American embassy, set back away from the thoroughfare, gleaming white with colonial columns in front of the main building and some smaller buildings among large oak trees on several acres of trimmed, neat grounds. The driveway was a sweeping curve that began at the boulevard a good hundred yards from the main building.

They passed on by and headed into one of the nicer residential districts.

Lyss noted that Julio was keeping an eye on the rear mirrors. Once in the residential area, they made several turns which obviously were unnecessary.

"Any sign of a tail?" Lyss asked.

"No," Julio answered, "but it doesn't cost anything to be sure."

They turned into a driveway of an expensive place and went around to the back, well out of sight of the road.

Julio went in through the back door without knocking. They passed into a large living room.

"I'm sorry it has taken us so long finally to meet, Juan," said the tall, rather heavy blond man who rose as Lyss entered. Julio had faded back toward the kitchen.

Lyss had known about George Overton for years and admired his past work, most of which had been done in the Philippines. As had been often the case in the agency, they had never met.

"It's a real pleasure to meet you at last, George. But it's not very pleasant in this disguise."

"Manila has been designated the base station for your field support," George said.

"Sarah Sanford and Josh Rosenbloom will arrive tomorrow afternoon. We are setting them up in a safe house not far from the wharf. It has complete communications equipment which can reach the Pharaon even if she goes as far south as Singapore. Our commo boys have set this up with the equipment Washington sent to us, but we will want Josh to check it all out."

George turned toward an arched entrance into the living area and added a false sense of drama to his voice.

"May I present Antoinette and Alfred Bennett?"

They walked into the room. Toni skipped across the rug into Lyss's arms. He embraced her and kissed both cheeks.

Al and Lyss shook hands, then embraced. It had been several years since they had seen each other on Lyss's West Virginia farm.

Alfred Bennett had been one of the heroes in the delta region during Tet '68, saving a village almost single-handedly. He was wounded severely and spent more than a month in Third Field Hospital in Saigon. He looked taller than his six feet because he was thin. His complexion was the dark and rough skin expected of a man who had been living mostly at sea for several years. He had met Toni during a tour in Algeria. She was a trim, pretty woman. The top of her close-cropped head came only to Al's shoulder.

"Sire," Al said, "your chariot is ready. We were short of wheels, so we put sails on her. The *Pharaon* is ready to go when you are. Of course, I hear some silly talk about new commo equipment as though I would sail the South Pacific without an adequate radio. I can't wait to work with that elephant Josh and see what his refinements are."

"Well, Al, I can tell you the main ingredients."

Lyss smiled.

"We are adding both scrambler and squirt capabilities."

"Are you carting that much junk in with you?" Al asked.

"No," Lyss said.

"I'll have a miniature squirt to use from the beach or nearby mountains to you, right? I understand they have really miniaturized it into a pack of cigarettes.

"The scrambler is strictly for communications between the *Pharaon* and George's base station here in Manila."

"I think the cocktail hour has arrived," George said. "Toni, what pleases your taste this evening?"

"I have acquired a number of Yankee habits, George."

Toni smiled.

"A dry martini, *s'il vous plait.*"

"For the last time...at least for a few weeks," Lyss said, "I will have my beloved scotch and water. Soon, I must start drinking like a Filipino."

As George busied himself at the bar, Lyss moved over to Al and began talking shop.

Lyss briefed Al on the general plan of putting Lyss ashore at Ninh Hoa just north of Nha Trang. From there he planned to walk up the mountains to Ban Me Thuot. He would take a bus to Dalat. Al agreed with the idea of exiting at Hoa Da, a tiny beach hamlet about fifty miles from Dalat. They agreed on seven days for planning to get from Manila to Ninh Hoa.

"If we have favorable winds," Al said, "we can count on a speed of about seven knots. After all, the *Pharaon* is a ketch, not a racing boat. Of course, if we have some bad weather it will affect our schedule. I've checked the weather. There's a big storm coming across, but if we're lucky, it will pass east of us.

"If we're not lucky, we might have to weather a big storm. I assure you, that's no fun. The route we'll follow is across open sea. Is there a specific time table we must use?"

"No," Lyss said, "I'm very anxious to get there and get this clambake cooking. Every hour that passes until I get Harvey away from those damned gooks is another hour he could be tortured or suffer in other ways."

George joined the conversation, suggesting that Sarah and Josh would need a few hours rest after their long flight. Lyss admitted he was overanxious but calmed down considerably.

"Josh is going to check out all the commo equipment," Lyss said. "He has a few gadgets to get for me from the embassy storeroom."

"Embassy storeroom, my royal ass," Al said with a snort. "What you mean is some technical devices you couldn't bring through customs."

"Sure. There must be a way to protect the old man."

They resumed the discussion. Lyss briefed Al on what was known about Harvey and his health. Lyss pointed out if Harvey was in bad condition it would add to the difficulties in getting Harvey from Dalat to the beach.

George suggested a meeting of all the principals at his house the day after tomorrow at noon, including lunch.

Lyss agreed.

"I'm very happy to do it all my way, but I didn't reach this ripe old age without knowing there were other ideas from other people that were, at least, worth considering."

George repeated the idea of a Thursday noon meeting.

Lyss said, "Fine. If it suits your plans, I'll arrange for Julio to get me here about eleven in the morning, ahead of the others."

"That will be fine," George said. "I'll see you here Thursday. Meanwhile, there's food on the table."

CHAPTER TEN

Most Filipinos were a fun loving people with an easy sense of humor, and, Lyss thought, most of them were square shooters. One of his sergeant instructors in the ROTC had been a Filipino, because in the period between World Wars I and II they were permitted to enlist in the regular U.S. Army and many did. They were good soldiers, quick to learn and crack shots. His trips to the Philippines had been all confined to the main island, Luzon. The capital of Manila was on Manila Bay.

South of Manila the remnants of an old volcano made a lake of exceptional beauty. Well north of Manila, high in the mountains, was the resort of Baguio, where the American Air Force maintained a popular resort for American military and government employees from all over East Asia.

Manila itself was a city of more than one and a half million people. Almost every race of the world was represented.

America had always been proud of being the

melting pot of the world, but if the U.S. was the world's melting pot, then the Philippines was the small melting pot of Asia.

Archeologists said it all began, probably in the ice age, when Negritos walked from Asia to the Philippines, then came Malays, Indonesians, Hindus and Chinese. Magellan found the islands in 1521.

Lyss had always admired Magellan more than any other early explorer. Columbus had dominated the American schoolroom. Ferdinand had drawn upon Christopher's discovery of South America to launch his plan to reach the Spice Islands by going west.

Magellan had announced he would go as far south as seventy five degrees if necessary to get around South America, but he discovered the straits that were named for him at fifty-four degrees. Little did he know the ice he would have encountered if he had gone fifteen degrees farther south.

Magellan set out with five ships September 20, 1519. After a stormy passage through the straits, he sailed into an ocean so calm he named it the Pacific. By March 16, 1521, Magellan reached Samar in the group of islands he named after St. Lazarus. When the Spanish took control in 1572 they named the islands the Philippines, after Philip II of Spain. Magellan landed on Cebu. He trusted the King of Cebu, who betrayed Magellan and had him killed in a battle on April 27, 1521. Then the King killed two other leaders of Magellan's party and only one ship, the Vittoria, made it around the world via the Cape of Good Hope to

Portugal, arriving with eighteen men as survivors.

But, by God, Lyss thought, *they had been the first to go all the way around the world.*

Soon the Spaniards began expeditions to the Philippines and remained in control there until they were defeated by the Americans in the Spanish-American war of 1898 in which Commodore Dewey crushed the Spanish fleet in Manila Bay.

The three centuries of Spanish influence and the Catholic Church dominated the ethnic values of the country. It was difficult to find a person in the Philippines of pure national origin. Most had the wide nose of the Negritos, the tawny colored skin of the Indonesians, and the languages of Spain and America.

If there was a typical race in the Philippines, it was the Tagalogs, whose language and physical attributes typified the racial mixture of the country. Most of the great native leaders had come from the Tagalogs from Aguinaldo to Magsaysay.

Lyss had often visited the great American military cemetery, erected by the Filipinos to honor the Americans who died on Corregidor, Bataan, or in death marches. The names of thousands of Americans were carved in the marble arches of the circular walkway around the cemetery. The beauty of the cemetery and the memory of those who had given their lives brought a lump to Lyss's throat.

Many of those "American" names were Filipinos who had served in the United States Army. Lyss felt it was fitting that he briefly return to Manila in the guise of a Filipino, a race he admired. They were good soldiers, faithful to both their native country and to America, their adopted country.

When he was there as an American, they had liked him as well.

Lyss was at loose ends most of the next day, anxiously awaiting the arrival of the two friends. He missed getting to see Sarah as soon as she arrived. Julio did report to him that the two had arrived and proceeded directly to the safe house.

Lyss took out his big suitcase and emptied it onto the bed. He had one of the collapsible cardboard suitcases made in England. It was reinforced with wood. The top telescoped down on the bottom, making it handily expandable.

It's for us middle class, Lyss thought. The rich folks had leather and the poor folks had cheap cardboard, nothing as sturdy as his bag.

Then he emptied out the few drawers of the dresser onto the bed and took inventory to be sure he had everything he needed for the trip to Vietnam.

In all his world travels, Lyss had learned to economize, carrying just enough clothes to get by and doing his own laundry in hotel lavatories. He had three pairs of boxer shorts, two T-shirts, four extra handkerchiefs, four pairs of black socks, three dress shirts, two white and one light blue, three Philippine shirts, one of which was long sleeved and required cuff links.   Two four-in-hand ties and one black bow tie, an extra belt, two extra pairs of trousers, one gray the other navy, one extra pair of shoes and the suit he was wearing.   His toilet articles included a Schick razor with extra blades, a can of Gillette Foam, a bottle of Vitalis, and a bottle of Mennen's Afta Shave, American products readily avaiable in Manila.

His small medicine kit had only aspirin, milk of magnesia tablets and Enterovioform tablets, some cotton swabs and four Band Aids.

He laughed.

"Something for a headache, something for constipation, and something for diarrhea."

Lyss felt he had all he needed, except he thought he ought to have a sweater, so he bought one.   It could get cool in the mountains of Dalat.

Of all his clothes and paraphenalia, only the sweater and his Philippine shirts had labels.   They were made in the Philippines.

In the event of his death from enemy action, Lyss did not want clothes' labels to disclose an American connection.

Then he ate a hearty supper, taken with a bottle of San Miguel, and slept like a baby with dry diapers.

In the morning, at the appointed hour, Julio delivered him and his baggage to the chief of station's house.   George was there to welcome him.

"I want to talk a bit, Juan," George said. "It is my sincere desire to do everything I can to help you in this mission, but damn it, it seems impossible even for a platoon of men, much less a man alone. Although, from the things I've heard of you, I'm sure if there is a person on earth who can do it, you're the one. No doubt that is why Campbell asked you to do it."

"Well, George, it may very well hinge on a lot of luck, like finding some of the old hands who helped us during the war. They are, naturally, a scarce item, but our intelligence in the area has remained good. There may be someone in Dalat who can help me.

"Then, too, I've talked a lot with Jim Shaw, who once was referred to as the mayor of Dalat. We have had some recent satellite pictures to help him in pointing things out to me. I have the advantage of having been a guest in the key house for several days immediately following the Tet battles.

"George, you know from a couple of your own experiences that often a singleton can get a lot done without exposure. If we tried to send in a platoon, we would have a pitched battle on our hands."

George poured fresh coffee and was about to agree with what Lyss had said when the doorbell rang and in walked Sarah beside the big Joshua Rosenbloom. Sarah and Lyss embraced and he gave her a friendly peck on the cheek. Josh's handshake was amazingly gentle for a person so large.

They were shortly followed by Al and Toni. The group moved into a room Lyss suspected was George's study. It had been converted into a conference room with a glass of water, a scratch pad and pencil at each of the six places.

George called upon Sarah, who was the senior case officer.

"There have been no new developments since Juan left Washington," she said. "We feel the plans and the timing as previously discussed are all valid. This would call for Juan to move on board this afternoon and for the *Pharaon* to sail at the discretion of her skipper in the morning.

"Well," Sarah smiled, "there is one slight change. Josh will remain here to assist whomever you assign from the station to the commo shack. I'll board the *Pharaon* and work with Al and Toni offshore."

Her plan did not raise an eyebrow because Sarah was known as a top professional in the business. Good case officers like to be as close as possible to the action in order to give the best possible support to the agents in the field.

Sarah had gained her position in the agency by hard work, good judgment and considerable luck. The men in the CIA did not always like to see a woman come to the top. Several old line chauvinists had been known to refuse a job when it meant a woman would be their supervisor. Most of the agency people, male and female, liked Sarah and respected her.

Josh outlined the communications check he would be making, indicating he could get it done in probably less than an hour with a good commo man from the station to help him.

"Juan," Josh's voice was subdued, "the gadgets come in the pouch. I'll bring 'em to the *Pharaon* tonight about chow time if you got somethin' to eat."

"There will be, you horse," Al said, "but don't eat as much as you look like you can."

They had a luncheon of chicken salad with no business transacted at the table. After the meal the three groups made separate departures.

As Lyss left, George gripped his hand, and said, "God be with you."

Julio took Lyss to the pier and carried his gear aboard and below deck. Lyss hoped he looked like a Filipino merchant with enough money to enjoy a little sailing trip.

Once on board, Lyss examined the *Pharaon*, which he knew Al had built in Taiwan. It was spotless, two cabins with a center saloon a landlubber would call a living room. On a vacation, a trip on this trim little ship would be great joy.

Josh was next on board, carrying Sarah's luggage, which he took below, along with the special gear he had for Lyss.

He started drilling Lyss on the use of the various gadgets.

DRAGONS YET TO SLAY

Josh laid out two fountain pens, one a ballpoint and the other a Parker 51. He explained the Parker 51 would not only write but would also fire a plastic .22 caliber bullet to stun an enemy rather than kill him.

The ballpoint handled one way would write and another became a hypodermic of knockout drops.

"Puncture a guy with this," Josh said, "and he's out in five seconds and flat on his ass for thirty minutes."

Any agent planning to go into enemy territory was supposed to carry a cyanide capsule with him to make suicide possible. Suicide was preferable to slow death by torture and insured no information was given to the enemy.

Lyss had always held it against Gary Powers that he did not take his capsule when his U-2 was shot down over Russia, causing great embarrassment to President Eisenhower and straining USSR-US relations.

Josh handed Lyss the capsule. Then Josh handed him what looked like a package of cigarettes.

"If you'll press here and talk to it, your voice is recorded," Josh said. "Press here and the recording speed is increased about ten times. Point it straight toward your target and press here and it is sent fer about ten miles."

"That's great, Josh," Lyss said. "It's much improved over the old model. You got anything that'll improve us old model agents?"

"I brung you one of the new airborne belt knives, complete with belt. The head looks like a belt buckle. Big difference between this one and the old ones is that it's made of special plastic. Better than the Ace of Spades I mentioned to you at the mansion and better than the fighting knives you used to know about, or did you?"

"Hell, Josh, I used one about twenty years ago in Arabia."

"Then here's the old Browning 9mm you wanted, with both plastic and conventional ammo. Why'd you have to tell Campbell about the special one I made fer you?"

"I didn't know you wanted it kept secret, Old Buddy. If you can't brag about your friends, who can you brag about?"

Unlike the new Browning, this one was thin. Lyss checked the magazine to find it only held seven rounds. The new Browning carried thirteen rounds but was much thicker.

Al, Toni, and Sarah all arrived shortly thereafter, and Lyss permitted himself an embrace, which Sarah returned with vigor.

"Here's your fortune, you pirate."

Sarah handed him a money belt which was heavy with gold. Lyss was a child when President Franklin Roosevelt had removed gold from the coinage during the great bank crisis of 1932. It was called going off the gold standard by economists. He recalled how a number of people hoarded what little gold they had, one of whom was his Yankee grandfather who had saddled him with the name Ulysses. Lyss's father had disapproved of gold hoarding so strongly that it was the first time Lyss remembered his father and grandfather arguing.

Gold, or money, had never been a god Lyss worshipped. He had done well financially. Other than security for himself and his family, it meant little to him.

The money belt of gold and his friends gathered together made Lyss realize that the project was imminent. Outwardly, he exuded confidence, but inwardly, he said to himself, *Lyss, this is the nut cutting, stop shaking and get going.*

Al said, "We'll go out after high tide about ten in the morning.

"Now in this basket is tonight's supper, which I believe will even satisfy the great Josh."

"In this sack," Sarah said, "are four bottles of a special California wine that even this fussy Filipino will like."

"Toni, can you fix up the chow?" Al said. "We need Sarah with us while we go up to the cockpit and check over the charts."

The four went to the cockpit. Al brought out several special charts of the South China Sea. Lyss pointed out Ninh Hoa, just north of Nha Trang, where he thought the entry could be conveniently made.

"It's well away from Cam Ranh Bay, keeping the Russians from being interested, and Nha Trang is farther north of Cam Ranh. The landing site is far enough away to keep the Vietnamese from seeing us," Lyss said.

They agreed that the return should be via Hoa Da. Lyss went into some detail about his walk up to Ban Me Thuot and some of his plans after he got to Dalat.

"One of the big problems for you and me, Al," Lyss said, "will be the scheduling. When you drop me on the hostile shore, I'll then suggest a time for us to be back in touch. If Harvey is not out, or is out but can't travel, we will have to set a second date. I think that is all you'll want to know at this time.

"It's hard to guess the day we'll be there, but I suggest about twenty-one days from the day I land, give or take a few days, about the twenty-ninth of the month."

"It looks okay to me. All you need is the endurance of a camel, the strength of an ox, and a hell of a lot of luck."

"It looks okay to me, too," Sarah said. "I like the idea of going in one place and coming out another. It's more secure."

"How about dinner?" Al said.

The saloon was replete with what some might have called a great picnic, but all would recognize as a sumptuous repast. Sarah broke out her special bottles of wine.

"Four of us drove out west this summer. We wound up in St. Helena touring great California wineries. At the Sutter Home Winery, that I was introduced to White Zinfandel. It took ingenuity to get it to Manila, I guarantee you.

"Here, one of you men open the first bottle."

"Well," said Josh as dinner ended. Two Chinese belches announced his favorable reception of the evening's food.

"I'm a fifth wheel on this vehicle what ain't got no wheels, so I'd better get back to my lonely couch.

"Besides," he smiled, "George is detailing one of his commo types to live there with me so we can monitor you twenty-four hours. They've finally let gals into commo, so I might have some compatible company."

The four of them toyed with their wine glasses, finishing up the second bottle. Lyss found he needed to find the "necessary" room. He knew Al had designed the boat, but he did not know whether it provided one or two heads.

He entered the cabin he knew was designated for him and was surprised to find both his and Sarah's luggage there.

She followed him and closed the door behind

her.

"I had a little private talk with Toni," Sarah said. "We agreed there was no use being coy about the bedroom situation. She said if you were asked publicly, you would probably sleep on the convertible couch in the saloon. Frankly, she was delighted when I told her we would share the same cabin. Any objections?" she asked, with a coy look.

Lyss took her in his arms and kissed her with such strength that she recoiled a bit.

"Do not damage the merchandise," she said. "I get your response, loud and ... ouch!"

Lyss found there was a private head in the cabin and indicated it to Sarah. She declined, and he entered. When he came back into the cabin, Sarah was gone and the door open. Back in the saloon, he found Toni and Sarah cleaning up the remains of the meal. He drained his wineglass.

Lyss went up on deck and found Al there, breathing in the air.

"It'll improve when we get out of the harbor. The South China Sea is one of the finest bodies of water, despite being cluttered up with a lot of those high rise ships the Chinese call junks.

"Lyss, the hell with that Juan stuff for what I want to say. Toni and I are delighted that you and Sarah have become good friends. Being alone is not my idea of real living, and Mattie's been gone for some time now. Damn it, you come back from this

Dragons Yet To Slay

mission of yours, you hear? If I thought it would enhance the chances of success, I'd go in with you. But along with others, I'm convinced the operation has the greatest chance of success with one man alone.

"Old Buddy, I don't have to tell you I think you can do it, and I think you're one of maybe a half dozen in the outfit who would have any chance of success."

Al embraced Lyss. There were tears in his eyes.

"I'm going into it with full information and with my eyes wide open, Al. I deeply appreciate what you've said. I'll do my best."

Sarah and Toni came up on deck and they gazed out at the lights of Manila.

Toni pointed.

"That's Corregidor over there, but your part of World War Two was over in another part of the world, wasn't it?"

"Yes, it was," Lyss said. "You were a little girl in Algiers when I helped liberate the town. Your papa once told me you were the darling of the American GI's in Algiers. Why weren't you in Oran when I was there?"

"Because, my love," she said saucily, "I was not old enough to fall in love with you. If you'd come back to Algeria ten years later, instead of going to Saudi Arabia, we might have become friends a lot sooner. I would have fallen madly in love with you, even if you were already taken."

"How can you run off such prattle and in English, too," Lyss said. "But, at last, you're in my clutches."

"Hands off," said Sarah, with gestures. "He's mine now."

There was a bit more banter, but, at last, Toni and Al said their good nights. Lyss and Sarah followed, each couple heading for their own cabins.

When all was quiet, Lyss told Sarah he was going on deck for a few minutes to do some thinking. About thirty minutes later, when he returned, he found Sarah in bed. He quickly took off his clothing and joined her. He caressed her gently, then pulled her body to his.

CHAPTER ELEVEN

They slept soundly. Sarah was awakened by the morning light. Sarah reached over to rub his hairy chest and then let her hand wander down. Lyss turned, and they made love again. Then they rose, washed, dressed and went into the saloon.

"We set sail in three hours, sailors," Al said.

They ate a hasty breakfast. Sarah left to go to the embassy for some final work. She said she would send a private word to Hamilton Campbell they were sailing today and everything was on schedule.

Josh came aboard and went over the communications equipment for a final time, with Al ever at his elbow. They did a radio check previously arranged with the Manila Station. As Josh put it, "All systems are go."

He went over the use of Lyss's miniature transmitter and squirt with both Al and Lyss. He pointed out that even without the squirt, the transmitter signal could not be intercepted except within a limited area.

Josh had barely left the boat when Sarah returned. She had chatted with Hamilton Campbell by teletype. He was pleased with the report. Ham had said there was no new information in headquarters. George sent a word of farewell and a strong message of good luck.

Al warmed up the engine. The loud purr assured Lyss the boat's engine was in fine tune.

Al ran up a couple of signal flags, radioed the harbormaster and they pulled away from the pier. There was a gentle breeze from the east. Shortly after getting his position, still in the harbor, Al hoisted the jib and mainsail. The *Pharaon* began to move out, running before the wind.

Lyss said his seagoing experience was limited.

"The nearest boat to this type were the boats we used for fishing off Chincoteague Island, Virginia," he said. "The next size I'm acquainted with was the passenger liner *Exeter* back in the days when she was plying the Mediterranean run from New York. So I guess you could say that my knowledge of boats goes from the ridiculous to the sublime."

"You'll learn fast," Al said.

They cleared the harbor. Al spread full canvas. They began a quiet, smooth movement through glassy water.

Lyss was with Al in the cockpit, admiring the skill of his old friend in handling a forty-seven foot boat.

"Toni is a pretty good helmsman," Al said, "but

it might be a good idea to break both you and Sarah into the basics. It isn't that difficult. Given time I'll bet you both would be great sailors. The work itself is not very demanding since we hoist and lower sails mechanically. Sometimes, like in a storm, we have to put up a special sail, but it's easy. We also tie down the big sails after they have been lowered in a storm."

Lyss began his learning process. Al was a good teacher. Lyss quickly learned about sailing downwind. Their course had been downwind since leaving Manila harbor. Al told him about sailing into the wind and tacking, but said it really would be best for him to learn by doing. Al discussed handling in a storm and promised later in the day to explain the sextant and electronic navigation.

Sarah and Toni came on deck. Lyss took Sarah midship. They leaned over to look at the water flowing smoothly by, with the bow creating beautiful foamy waves. The sea was remarkably smooth. Al warned this probably meant they were going to get into the approaching storm. The weather forecast said it was due in from the south.

Al and Toni joined them.

"Who's minding the store?" Lyss asked.

"Oh, I just put it on automatic when we're going so steady. It's a good idea for someone to remain topside to watch at all times, though. If you wish, we'll take turns. If I'm below and you see something, you can give me a holler.

"My gut tells me we're going to have some fairly heavy weather either tonight or tomorrow, so we'd better take it as easy as possible. We surely won't get much rest if we have a strong wind."

"I don't know about sailing," Lyss said, "but I've learned to play my hunches. Before we bed down tonight, I suggest we batten down."

"It's so nice now," Sarah said, "I think I'll go down and bring up a tray of coffee. Would anybody prefer tea? Toni says I'd better learn to work in the galley. Al says I must learn to sail. Juan, the pirate, has things for me to do. Oh, well, even if we are on serious business, we might as well enjoy it."

She returned in a few minutes with a tray, cups, a pot of coffee and a plate of cookies. They enjoyed the mid-morning snack as the tropical sun began to warm their backs.

"As we cruise around the South Pacific," Al said, "we mostly have beautiful weather like this because we pull into a port when there's a storm or even a high wind. We don't have that choice on this voyage because it's open sea from the Philippines to the Vietnam coast. If there's work to do, this is the time to do it."

Lyss went below and pulled out the nautical charts and his detailed map of the central part of South Vietnam. He had always thought of Manila as being well north and east of Vietnam. Now he could see they were going almost eight hundred miles west and less than a hundred south to get to

Ninh Hoa. He suddenly realized how different going somewhere by boat was from flying. Sailing, you had a better sense of direction.

It was smooth sailing most of the day. Toni joined Al in the cockpit. Sarah and Lyss went to the saloon for soup and sandwiches, then returned to the cockpit. Al and Toni went down for food. Then the girls stripped to bikinis and lay on deck to soak in the tropical sun.

Late in the evening when the sun was sinking, Al secured the helm again. All four gathered in the cockpit for cocktails. Lyss restricted himself to beer. It was a jovial session. Then Sarah and Toni brought up plates of food and a bottle of Australian wine for a festive supper.

Not long after sunset, Al asked Lyss to take the helm. "I'm going below for a bit of sleep," he said.

"It'll be good for you to get the feel of the helm. I'll come up about midnight, earlier if you call me. That bright, almost blue star hanging over the bow is Venus. She's a good marker for you. If it clouds up, your magnetic course is two hundred and forty degrees. I find it easier to steer by the stars than the compass."

Sarah came into the cockpit and seated herself beside Lyss. He held her close. She leaned her head against his shoulder. Conversation did not seem necessary. Lyss's mind was on the coming days, but he enjoyed the present as well.

Lyss pondered the problems he might soon he facing. Would the people of the new regime in Vietnam be against or accept a Filipino construction supervisor? Would he be recognized as a Filipino? Would his long walk up to Ban Me Thuot raise any questions from people who saw him on the highway? Would he find Harvey where he was reported to be?

The sky began to be overcast about ten o'clock. The midnight hour came quickly. He was surprised when Al touched his shoulder. Lyss and Sarah went below and to their bunk.

The gentle sounds of the sea were a sedative. They both slept soundly until the boat began to make extra movements. Lyss looked at his watch. It was three o'clock. He dressed, including rain gear and went up on deck to join Al in the cockpit.

He found Al had lowered and secured all sails, except a small, stout, triangular sail near the top of the mainmast.

"That's called a try sail," Al said. "It enables me to keep the boat on the course I select in a storm. The wind is coming directly out of the south, so I've turned into it a bit. It's best to be off the wind about sixty degrees, so our course isn't affected that much, but our speed is.

"The sea can be an all consuming dragon. She breathes water instead of fire. She tests your strength, your skills, and above all else, your will to resist her."

He handed the wheel over to Lyss.

"Just hold her steady. I'm going to get out the shield."

Al rummaged in a locker next to the cockpit and came up with some steel rods and canvas. Very soon he had the windbreaker up to protect the cockpit.

He brought out two web harnesses and ropes, with huge snaps on them and told Lyss to snap one on his safety harness.

"If it really gets rough, this will either keep you from going overboard or enable you to get back aboard. I think it's going to start pouring here in a little bit."

The wind blasted at the boat. The waves reached higher. The *Pharaon* pitched high as it hit a wave. Then it plunged down into the trough between waves. The deluge began. Water in great amounts struck the boat and Al and Lyss, despite their cover. It was almost impossible to see through the shield, but Al, showing great strength, held the boat on the course he had chosen.

Then a rope lashing the mainsail to the boom broke loose. Lyss set out to tie it up.

Holding to anything he could find, he worked his way forward, very slowly, then reached the boom, which was slashing back and forth. He managed to get to the rope which had come loose and was reaching for it when the boat heaved, the boom spun at him and dashed him overboard into the turblent sea.

He went under the water. The force of the

waves swept him to the stern. His safety line became taut and yanked at him like some giant pulling in a fish.

Coming to the surface, he got his breath and began to pull himself hand over hand to the boat. Each time the boat went over a wave, the rope yanked at him so hard he was sure either his ribs or the rope would break.

Lyss felt as strong a fear as he had ever felt in his life. He wondered if it would be this violence of nature that would stop his mission.

He kept pulling his way along the rope and finally reached the side of the boat, hauled himself up on deck, then into the cockpit, where he fell to the deck, exhausted.

"You all right?" Al said.

"Just beat to death, Al. I'll make it in a minute or two."

When he was able to stand, Al had him take the helm and stayed with him to guide him for several of the pitches and dives. Then Al went forward himself to lash the boom securely.

On his return, he resumed the helm, telling Lyss to lie on the deck of the cockpit and rest.

"You don't have to coax me," Lyss said.

Then except for brief moments, Al kept the helm.

About noon the rain ceased and the wind decreased, but the waves remained heavy.

"If you will be careful, I think you can go below and check up on Toni and Sarah. Toni knows they should stay below. See if you can find a couple of mugs of coffee. You can lace mine with a bit of brandy. Keep your safety line on."

Lyss went below and found Sarah and Toni in the saloon. He excused himself and went into the cabin and changed clothes. Bringing out the soaked clothing, he reported on conditions. His brief report of his own dangerous episode brought gasps from Sarah and Toni. He asked Toni for coffee. Without asking Lyss, she reached into one of the lockers and poured a generous shot of brandy into Al's cup, then looked up at Lyss and laced his cup when Lyss nodded.

Back in the cockpit, Al and Lyss savored the hot coffee and brandy and felt warmth coursing through their veins.

"We'll see stars tonight," Al said. "It'll smooth out a bit tomorrow. I doubt if we'll have any more days like yesterday."

The rain had stopped, the wind diminished, but the waves were still high.

"Lyss, do you think you could handle the helm for a couple of hours?" Al asked. "I'm bushed. I need some rest. Call me if you run into something unusual."

Al went below. In a few minutes, Sarah came to the cockpit and stood beside Lyss, holding him closely.

"I could have lost you, lover," she said with a quiver in her voice. "In the midst of this awful rain and blasting wind and high waves, it could have been all over."

He put his free arm around her, reached down and kissed her cheek. She turned and lifted her lips to his.

The waves eased a bit. Lyss was able to sit down in the cockpit. They held each other close. Time passed swiftly. Al returned and Lyss looked at his watch. It was a few minutes before midnight.

Lyss and Sarah went to the saloon. Toni's door was shut.

They entered the room. She reached up to kiss him again.

As he kissed her, Lyss pulled her body close to his, then he backed away enough to reach the buttons of her blouse, which he began to unfasten. She began undoing the buttons of his shirt.

Then he reached under the loose blouse to her back and unfastened her bra.

They let the clothes fall to the deck and embraced again. He carefully laid her on the bed. They made love.

By mid-afternoon the next day, the sea had calmed down a bit to wide, gentle swells.

In his happiness about the night before, Lyss began to think of what a new life might be like with

Sarah.   He lay down on the forward deck and began to dream of the future.

Then his thoughts went back to his first trip to Saigon and one of the greatest events in his past life, his work in Saigon during the great Tet Offensive of 1968.

DRAGONS YET TO SLAY

CHAPTER TWELVE

Lyss thought of his departure from Washington in 1967 and the long, restless flight. PanAm Flight 841 was called the red-eye by the military and the civilians who took the forty hour journey to Vietnam with no rest.

It was Sarah Sanford who met him at the airport and took him almost immediately to Hamilton Campbell's home for a dinner with the key officers of the station. Ham was CIA's Chief of Station in Saigon then.

Campbell conducted only one piece of business at the dinner.

"My purpose in gathering you here tonight is to introduce Colonel Ulysses McCutcheon, who will be my chief of staff. When he speaks to you, it will be with my authority, so pay attention."

To Lyss it seemed the dinner dragged on forever. It had been more than forty hours since he had slept.

It was to be the second time Lyss would work directly under Ham, the first being when Ham was a division chief in Washington.

When Lyss was finally so weary he could hardly stand, Ham excused him. Lyss went to the hotel for his first night's sleep in Vietnam.

The next day he reported in at the old Embassy near the Saigon River. He was in uniform as a colonel, U.S. Army. He had worked hard for uniform and rank.

"This chief of staff thing is new to me, Ham," Lyss said. "What are my duties?"

"Anything I want you to do."

In carrying out Ham's orders, Lyss had no difficulty with the division chiefs, several of whom were senior in civilian rank to Lyss.

In November, 1967, the new embassy was opened.

One of Lyss's responsibilities was to assign and supervise the duty officer who would spend the night in the office on the sixth floor of the new embassy. It was customarily a boring night spent on a cot next to the phone and the Garnet Net two way radio.

On the afternoon of January 30, 1968, on Ham's instructions, eight people met with Lyss in the conference room. They were the working level representatives of the intelligence arms of every American service in country. They discussed the current Viet Cong positions, strengths and capabilities. It was obvious the Cong were poised for an attack.

"Good intelligence can give you the strength, location, and capabilities of your enemy," Lyss said. "But we need to look into a crystal ball to decide their intentions.

"You gentlemen are today's crystal ball.

"We know the Cong is poised and capable of a widespread attack. We have alerted the ARVN and the police to this. The question is: Will they attack during the sacred days of Tet?"

Tet was the holiest of the Buddhist holidays, corresponding to the Chinese New Year. It was the custom for the Vietnamese to return to the towns of their origins for three days of parties and eating and worship. Under normal circumstances the ARVN and the police would operate on those three days with only skeleton strength, permitting the vast majority to return home for their celebrations. This year, with the warning of the impending attack, units were down to only half strength.

In the discussion at Lyss's meeting, most agreed that the Cong would not attack during the holy days, but would begin the battle very soon thereafter. Lyss put it to a vote. It was eight to one that they would not attack during Tet.

One of the participants was Matthew MacAlister, an old friend of Lyss's who represented J-2 of MACV at this meeting. His was the lone dissenting vote.

Matt MacAlister had been a weapons platoon

leader in Lyss's rifle company before Pearl Harbor. When the events of December 7, 1941, took place, there was a frantic call from military headquarters for officer candidates. Lyss sent Matt to OCS where he became an officer, had a fine record and stayed in the Regular Army. Now he was a colonel. They were delighted to be serving together again.

After the meeting adjourned, Matt came to Lyss.

"Damn it, Lyss, I just feel it in my bones those fuckers are going to attack tonight."

"I cannot put out an intelligence estimate on the feelings in your bones, Matt," Lyss said.

Lyss returned to his house, which he shared with Clifford Thurmond, a retired major general in Vietnam under contract to CIA. That night they had a small dinner for a visiting chief of station and one of his officers. Lyss's servants were gone for the holidays, so Sarah cooked the dinner.

They had finished dinner and the guests had departed. Lyss took Sarah back to her apartment, then called Horace Oliver, the duty officer. Because of the tense situation, Lyss had placed two other officers with Horace to assist him if needed.

They reported a negative. Everything was quiet. It was eleven o'clock so Lyss dismissed the two officers and told them to go home.

Sound asleep, Lyss was startled out of bed by a blast from his radio. It was three o'clock in the morning.

"Garnet Five, the embassy is under attack!"

Lyss could hear heavy explosions and small arms fire.

The CIA offices on the sixth floor of the embassy did not have blackout curtains. Lyss told Oliver to place his microphone and a telephone on the floor, turn out the lights and lie down on the floor. The angle at which the VC had to shoot thus kept him out of the line of fire.

"Repeat all your messages to me, Horace. I will keep your log," Lyss said.

The window shutters of the better French designed homes provided a natural blackout. Lyss was on the second floor. In a few minutes he heard small arms fire and explosions somewhere near the house. Lyss set himself up at the radio to keep in touch and keep the log. Then Clifford came in.

Lyss recalled some excerpts from the log.

Jeremy Marshall, police liaison, reported the Korean embassy near Independence Palace was under fire.

At 0315, Garnet Eight, who lived in an apartment just north of the embassy reported.

"There is a firefight taking place in front of the embassy. There have been some explosions in Norodom."

Norodom was the one story annex east of the

embassy building where the consul general had his office. There were also some CIA offices there.

Cliff reported small arms fire near the house with a heavy explosion about a hundred yards away. Lyss learned later this was at the residence of the Philippine ambassador.

Jeremy Marshall reported a house under construction, near the Korean embassy, had been taken over by VC. They were sniping from it. The Korean embassy was just north of the palace.

Cliff and Lyss heard shots in their yard twice before 0400. At 0410 Garnet Commo on the fourth floor said a Marine in Norodom was believed dead. He further reported another Marine from the first floor had been wounded and had been brought up to the fourth floor.

About 0415 Jeremy said the police report was that two truckloads of VC had entered the city. One was headed for the embassy.

"Garnet Control," Lyss said, "tell him they have arrived."

Garnet Commo told Lyss headquarters wanted a report. Lyss suggested a brief message: "Embassy is in friendly hands."

The wounded Marine being treated on the fourth floor said the first floor of the embassy was a shambles.

At 0437 the wounded Marine was taken to the roof chopper pad, but there was no chopper there.

At 0510 all branch chiefs were instructed to

get word to as many of their people as possible to stay in their quarters until the damage to the embassy could be assessed. The attack continued.

At 0525 a chopper tried to land to evacuate the Marine from the embassy roof. Small arms fire from the VC in the embassy yard kept the chopper from landing.

The guard at Lyss's house reported two bodies in the street in front of the house, apparently shot by the military police. Cliff slung his carbine on his shoulder and went to investigate.

Cliff reported one Nung guard had left and the other was scared shitless. Lyss told Cliff to tell the other guard to go home.

"We will defend ourselves."

At 0546 the chopper tried to land at the embassy, but was again driven off.

At 0625 Garnet Commo said MACV had ordered infantry to the embassy and expected them to arrive about 0645.

The chopper tried for the third time at 0640 to land on the embassy roof and again was driven off by small arms fire.

At 0702 Cliff took over Lyss's radio to give him a short break.

The chopper finally landed at 0707. It left some ammunition for the Marines and evacuated the wounded Marine.

The infantry arrived at the embassy at 0720. The battle became intense, but, as Lyss recalled, it was short. Nineteen Viet Cong bodies were found on the yard of the embassy.

Some American soldiers passed by Lyss's house and removed the two VC bodies.

Jeremy Marshall made a fairly comprehensive report at 0730. He said there had been attacks in the area of Saigon radio, National Palace, American embassy, Circle Sportif, Tu Duc, and Li Quang (Cholon) police substations. The chief of police expected to lose Li Quang. His report indicated the attacks were by several hundred VC calling themselves the Saigon Liberation Front.

Horace was called by Garnet Commo to come to the fourth floor and talk to Washington on the teletype at 0825 hours.

Then about 0830, Lyss and Cliff moved to Walton Edson's nearby house.

Garnet Control reported at 0850 hours that an Army officer was searching the embassy for explosives.

Lyss said, "that's stupid. The VC never got in the embassy to plant explosives or anything else."

Lyss, Cliff and Walton Edson called Ham for permission to go to the embassy. Ham denied the request. He said he was asking for an escort of military police and would come by and pick the three up.

DRAGONS YET TO SLAY

At 1030 hours Lyss and his friends entered the embassy.

Thus began the three most critical weeks of Lyss's life. Although never in serious danger, he traveled armed whenever he was not in the embassy. He spent most of these three weeks in the embassy.

He averaged about four hours sleep a night for the first ten days. Ham put him in charge of the night shift. The station was open twenty-four hours a day. General Chandler Boone, the commanding general of MACV, issued a strict curfew from 1800 to 0700 hours, so Lyss and a skeleton crew ran things from 1730 to 0730 hours. Ham and the regulars would come in at 0730. Lyss was the prime speaker at the early morning staff meeting, briefing on the night's activity and the cable traffic from headquarters. It was during Lyss's shift that it was working hours in Washington, so he had to answer most of the priority cable traffic.

After he finished his briefing, he would go to his desk for his regular work. Then about 1130 hours Lyss would go home for a nice lunch, which his household crew would fix for him. He would bathe, shave and go to bed in his own bed, usually for two or three hours. Then he would put on a clean uniform and get to the embassy office by 1600 hours. Ham would brief him on the day's activities and then, about 1730, turn the station back over to Lyss.

Ham had both radio and telephone communication at home. If something critical came up, Lyss would call Ham on the phone and "double talk" the message.   If it was serious enough, Ham would call for the military police escort required during curfew hours and come to the embassy. As Lyss recalled it, this only happened twice in three weeks.

During the evening hours the duty group had plenty of coffee and old fashioned World War II C-Rations. Lyss raised hell and demanded the tanker's ration. It was called fifteen-in-one and was far superior to C-Rations. As General Boone was an old tanker himself, he laughed when he heard Lyss's request and ordered top priority on it.

When the evening quieted down, Lyss would lie down on the couch and often get some sleep.

One night, having dozed off, he was suddenly awakened by the crash of shells and the popping of small arms fire.

He jumped from the couch and went out to the central room to find that Joshua Rosenbloom had brought in a tape of the Garnet Net broadcast during that critical first night and played it. Josh and Lyss had been friends several years, but Lyss said his first desire was to cut that huge Jew into chunks and feed him to any handy group of buzzards.

Lyss was given medals by both General Boone and by the CIA for his work during this time.

Lyss later told some friends he felt that in those three weeks he had given his greatest service to his country in twenty seven years of service.

"Think how good I would have looked if I had put out an intelligence estimate on the basis of the feeling in Matt MacAlister's bones."

Two thoughts were always major in his mind after Tet '68. The first was that Tet was a tremendous victory for the Americans and for the ARVN.

The Viet Cong, under the banner of the Saigon Liberation Front, had expected the people of Saigon to rise up and welcome them as liberators, but the people made it clear the Viet Cong were not welcome.

The media in Washington and New York played it as a defeat and beat the drums of withdrawal loudly.

The other consuming thought recurred as often as the picture would be repeated in some book or some news article on a Tet '68 anniversary. That was the picture of General Nguyen Ngoc Loan, chief of South Vietnam's National Police, blowing the brains out of a Viet Cong's head. None of the stories, Lyss recalled bitterly, ever told the full story. General Loan had just been told that this was the VC who had killed one of Loan's police associates and then murdered that associate's wife and little children. Nor did any of the stories tell that Loan had been without sleep for forty-eight hours. One picture did show him reclining on the pavement during the bitter conflict.

Tet '68 was a major victory, and General Loan was a great hero.

Lyss was awakened from his reverie by Al coming forward on deck just to check up on him.

On the seventh night out, anticipating the next day would bring them into sight of Vietnam, Lyss and Sarah made passionate love as though to make up for the days and nights ahead when they would be apart.

In mid-afternoon of the eighth day out of Manila, Al lowered the sails and deployed the sea anchor.

"We will lay out here until dark. With the sails down, we are less visible. I am surprised we have seen no aircraft today. We are right under the commercial flight path from Singapore to Hong Kong."

As though someone heard Al, a jet leaving a contrail high in the sky made its way north.

Lyss spent a considerable time picking out the clothing he could take in his backpack. He dressed in a suit with shirt and tie. Then he picked out another suit and shirt, some underclothes, a jumpsuit for a work garment, two Philippine shirts and an extra pair of shoes and his toilet articles. He packed only one blanket, hoping the mountain nights would not be too cold until he surfaced where there were hotel facilities. He carefully packed his duffle together into a medium sized backpack. To all intents and purposes, he looked like a mountain climber, except for his jacket and tie.

Darkness came. The *Pharaon* sailed due west and about ten o'clock light were seen to the southwest.

"That is Nha Trang," Al said. "We'll head on toward shore.   I will get out the inflatable raft. We will row to the beach.

"Coming back, I will use the quiet motor. Once back on board, I will head out to sea about twelve miles off shore.   I want to be out of sight from the hills behind the beach.

"I'll pull back to about four miles offshore tomorrow night at ten o'clock. If you have not left the beach or have an emergency, give me our agreed signal.

"If I don't get your signal, I'll head out to sea and meet our other prearranged rendezvous on the twenty-ninth."

"That's all A-okay with me," Lyss said.

Sarah had come on deck. She looked confused. She was toying with a piece of string, running it through her fingers.

"I don't know what to say, Lyss my love."

"Just be here when I get back, Sarah," Lyss said.

The *Pharaon* was less than a thousand yards from the beach when Al launched the raft. They both entered it. Both paddled vigorously. They reached the shore in only a few minutes.

Lyss jumped out.

"Many thanks, Old Buddy," he said in a soft voice.

"I will see you on schedule."

"Break a leg, Lyss," Alfred whispered, and started the boat back toward the *Pharaon.*

Lyss waded the short distance to the sandy beach, wiped his feet, put on his socks and shoes, then walked up into the trees that lined the beach. He was back on Vietnamese soil.

DRAGONS YET TO SLAY

CHAPTER THIRTEEN

The secret arrival across the sandy beach was quite a change from his first time in Vietnam. At that time he had come through Tan Son Nhut Airport wearing a colonel's uniform. He was welcomed and respected as a part of the American army. His ostensible purpose was to help save the South Vietnamese from the Communists. Now he was only an ordinary Filipino contractor seeking employment.

The beach was rather narrow at the point of landing. It had only thirty feet or so of sand. Lyss walked to the line of pines and bamboo and tried to get through the dense bamboo.

He came back to the sand and began looking for a path off the beach, which he was sure existed. From his map study, he knew he was not much more than a quarter mile from the coastal highway north of Nha Trang.

It was quite dark, but as he walked parallel to the tree line, he discovered a path leading through the trees. He wanted to get off the beach and to the highway. He knew it should not be far. In a few minutes he came upon it.

Should he turn left or right? He should be near the junction of the Ban Me Thuot highway with the coastal highway.

He did not want to get too close to Nha Trang so decided to turn north. Luck was with him. In a few more minutes he came upon the highway junction and headed west. A dilipidated sign at the junction pointed west twenty-five kilometers to Khanh Duong. He took off at a steady pace.

Lyss was looking for a nice patch of woods near the highway, which would provide him shelter for a few hours sleep. Too many questions might be asked of a man walking at night.

The moon rose behind him. He was grateful it was only a half moon, but it gave considerable light. After walking about two hours, Lyss estimated he had made a little better than nine kilometers. He came upon a canal. To the right he saw a small group of pine trees interlaced with bamboo. He entered and found soft, clean ground.

He woke at dawn. He washed his face in the canal, then reached into his pack for a handful of the nuts and raisins mixture he had brought as trail rations. After two good drafts of water from his canteen, he resumed him walk west on the highway.

It was his first good look at Vietnam after a six-year absence and a complete change in government.

DRAGONS YET TO SLAY

While he had never been in this specific coastal area, he had been at several points along the coast north of Saigon. He found the paving substantially as he remembered it. Perhaps there were a few more pot-holes, but the lush green grass and the lovely pine and bamboo were still there. It made him optimistic.

The land had not changed much. Perhaps the real people of the country had not altered their point of view much either. It was in the cities and the centers of government that changes were made. Cultures of the past had not died out easily. The human spirit had prevailed.

He walked steadily, but without pressure. He knew such a pace would take him five kilometers an hour, maybe a little less.

After two hours of walking, he saw a young boy driving a water buffalo along the highway. He stopped and spoke to the boy in Vietnamese.

"Where is your house, nephew?"

"In Khanh Duong," the boy said respectfully.

"Is there public transportation from there to Ban Me Thuot?"

"There is a bus on Fridays, if it pleases them to drive that day."

"Then I guess I will keep walking," Lyss said with a smile.

The boy said, "You will be more likely to get to Ban Me Thuot this week."

"Is there a place to eat in Khanh Duong?"

"A small cafe. The noodles are good."
"Then I shall stop there."

The beast had been nibbling at some grass by the side of the road. The boy whacked him with a long, thin bamboo shoot, and they headed on east.

Lyss resumed his walk, pleased he did not seem to have aroused any curiosity in the mind of the boy.

The variety of ethnic backgrounds of the Vietnamese people had caused them to have a variety of accents, Lyss thought.   Accent itself had not been a barrier to discussion.

After taking another handful of his raisins and nuts and a healthy draft from his canteen, he headed again toward Khanh Duong. He was surprised at the complete lack of traffic on the road, but no traffic diminished the possibility he might be stopped by some passing motorist and asked difficult questions.

It was about an hour and a half before he sighted Khanh Duong in the edge of the mountains. It was fifteen more minutes before he was walking down the main street. He saw a cafe sign and stopped. It was a small room with only four tables. One wall had a large picture of Ho Chi Minh. Another wall was covered with shelves loaded with glasses, cups and dishes. There was no counter as you would find in America.

He took a seat at one of the tables. A young Vietnamese woman came to him.

"I understand you serve good noodles," he said.

"We do, indeed," the young woman said, "but today we have soup Chinoise, if you would enjoy that."

It was one of Lyss's favorite dishes. The big steaming bowl of chicken broth with bits of fish and shrimp and clear noodles was delicious.

"Is there public transportation to Ban Me Thuot?" he asked.

"Only on Fridays. Not always then."

"How far is it?"

"About eighty kilometers."

"Do many people walk the distance?"

Her advice was to walk if he wanted to be sure to be in Ban Me Thuot this week. He then bought a loaf of bread from her and again headed west on the highway. There still was no traffic for quite a while. There were more slopes up than down over the rugged terrain.

Lyss passed the edge of a rushing mountain stream in mid-afternoon. Then he saw his first vehicle since leaving Khanh Duong. He was surprised. It was an American Ford sedan in fairly good repair. He guessed it was only about five years old.

Lyss was worried about such a good car. Its driver could only be a man of influence in the new regime.

"You, there," the driver said with authority in

Vietnamese. "Where are you going?"

"To Ban Me Thuot to see if there is business I can transact. There is no bus until Friday. It does not always run," Lyss replied.

"If I am lucky and stay in good health, I will get there tomorrow, or perhaps the next day."

"Let me see your papers."

"Certainly, sir."

Lyss handed him his passport and entry papers.

"Since you came to Ho Chi Minh City, where have you been?"

"First to Bien Hoa, then to Nha Trang. I am seeking work in supervising construction, but there does not appear to be much the new regime desires to be built. I am also good at supervising remodeling."

"We do not need you Filipinos here," the man said, vigorously crushing a cigarette in the car's ashtray.

"We can handle our own construction."

"Your government permitted me to come. I not only need the work, but I am quite good at what I do."

"Well," his face lost some of its sternness, "go on to Ban Me Thuot. If you want to work bad enough to walk that far, maybe you can serve our country. When you get to Ban Me Thuot, go to the government building and ask for Nha. He might have something for you. Tell him you talked to Nguyen Van Hai."

"Thank you very much, sir," Lyss said. "I will be sure to do that."

The car headed on east. Lyss began his uphill walk. He estimated he had come about fifteen kilometers since lunch, and thus had about thirteen to fifteen hours of walking ahead of him.

He decided to stop at the first decent camping site.

The ground was rougher and rockier. There were fewer bamboo but more pines than at lower levels. The air was cool. Lyss knew the night would be cold. If he could find cover in a secluded place off the road, he would build a fire.

He walked rather briskly, keeping the blood circulating. He knew he was making good time, even in the mountains. About an hour after his encounter with the new regime, he found a swift little brook flowing by the road, then under the road through a culvert. Several hundred yards from the road, he saw a group of pines he thought would offer cover.

He moved to the trees and began making camp. He built a small fire from deadwood he found nearby, pulled a can of beans from his pack and a small pot in which to warm them.

It tasted good. He rested in front of the fire while it was still daylight. He would not have the fire at night because it would be too visible to patrols on the highway.

He pulled out his blanket, wrapped it about

him, and was soon fast asleep.

He slept well, despite the cold night and re-sumed his journey without incident.

Lyss again camped by the roadside the third night. On the fourth day he arrived in Ban Me Thuot about noon. He found a small red brick hotel and slept for nearly eighteen hours.

Mid-morning the next day, he went to the government building, seeking Nha. He waited in an outer office for nearly an hour before being shown into Nha's presence.

Much to Lyss's amazement, it was General Tran Quoc Nha. General Nha had on several occa-sions been a dinner guest in Lyss's house in Saigon.

General Tran Quoc Nha was one of the final characters in the play of the last days of South Vietnam and American participation. He had been a key staff officer to both Nguyen Cao Ky and Nguyen Van Thieu during their administrations.

When General Duong Van Minh had taken over the final shambles, he asked General Nha to try to negotiate with the Provisional Revolutionary Govern-ment. He did his best, but with about as much success as a mouse negotiating with a vicious cat.

While his critics considered General Nha inde-cisive and often ineffective, there was one area in which no one questioned him. He was a loyal, faithful Vietnamese. When offered evacuation at the same time as other high officials, he had refused.

"I am Vietnamese. This is my country. I cannot leave it."

The last Lyss had heard of him, he had been imprisoned by the North Vietnamese conquerors. It was startling to see him in a position of considerable responsibility in the new regime. He now appeared to be a province chief, if the new regime used such titles.

Tran Quoc Nha was in close touch with agency personnel throughout almost all of his late career, but he also maintained a type of independence. Lyss had never been one of those intimate with him, but he had hosted several dinners where General Nha was an honored guest.

Lyss as Juan Farrar made his pitch for construction work to General Nha. He did not seem to get his full attention. Lyss spoke only in Vietnamese. He knew General Nha was fluent in English. Even with Lyss speaking in Vietnamese, General Nha appeared to notice something.

"Mr. Farrar," he said, "there is something most familiar about you, but I cannot place it. Have we met before?"

Lyss's first real conversation with someone who knew both Americans and Filipinos revealed something in Lyss that could not be explained. Lyss worried this might shatter the plan. Nha was never anti-American. Lyss decided he would just have to weather the storm.

"I do not think so, sir," Lyss said. "Most certainly I have heard of you and your great patriotism, but I really did not know when Nguyen Van Hai sent me to Nha he was sending me to a person of your stature."

"Thank you for your kind remarks. May I see your papers?"

Lyss handed him his passport, deciding to wait to see if General Nha wanted other papers.

General Nha examined the passport and turned to Lyss.

"There are a few small mistakes in your entry visa. These might cause some difficulty with certain people. If you will leave your passport with me until tomorrow, I will see that it is correct."

"Thank you very much. I am here to help the new regime if my knowledge of building can be of any use."

Lyss left the government building and returned to his hotel. He was disturbed at the session with General Nha and particularly that his disguise might be flawed.

We made no effort to change the voice, Lyss thought. *Maybe we should have.*

In many countries it was routine to find a small error in a passport, or find some other excuse, in order to keep it overnight, so it could be photographed for the files.

Still restless after dinner, he had trouble getting to sleep.

He woke about one o'clock in the morning and felt moisture on his face. His hand came away bloody, so he hurried into the bathroom and washed with cold water. His left nostril was pouring blood.

He took one of the bath towels to hold over his nose and went to his knapsack to get out the Noz-Stop and vaseline. Quickly, he covered the rubber with vaseline, slipped it into the nostril, then took his hypodermic air pump and inflated the two ends of the Noz-Stop, one deep in the nostril, the other near the exit. He removed the hypo, washed his face and watched a few minutes to see that the bleeding was blocked.

Then he cleaned up the bed with a cold, wet washcloth and went back to sleep. The test of effectiveness would be in the morning.

After a few hours sleep, he got up and carefully deflated and removed the Noz-Stop. The bleeding had stopped with appropriate clotting in the nostril.

That was a close call, Lyss thought. He had to avoid blowing his nose for a couple of days.

Promptly at ten o'clock, he returned as scheduled to General Nha's office.

"Ah, good morning, Mr. Farrar. It is good to see you again. Here is your passport. I believe it is now flawless. Have you made any additional plans?"

"Yes, sir," Lyss said. "I have decided to take the bus to Dalat this afternoon. If I can find a comfortable house there, I may make Dalat my headquarters. I like Dalat and its climate, not to mention its great strawberries, which should soon be available. If you hear of work here or in Pleiku that I can perform, I trust you will call on me.

"Your kindness in straightening out my passport is especially appreciated. Perhaps if you come to Dalat soon, I can express my appreciation in a better way."

"When you get to Dalat," Nha said, "give my regards to Vo Van Son. He might be of some help to you, particularly in finding a house that would suit you."

Lyss was glad to have this excuse to look up the man he had intended as an early contact.

He decided General Nha was treating him as a friend. There was no doubt expressed in his voice.

In any event, Lyss was disturbed and felt it was best he get on to Dalat, where he had much to do.

Then he set out to equip himself for the trip to Dalat.

CHAPTER FOURTEEN

Lyss went into one of the stores in Ban Me Thuot and found two fairly good used leather suitcases with brass fasteners and straps. He resisted the idea of getting the common cardboard ones, because as a good Filipino businessman he should appear successful.

He had no difficulty packing the clothes, toilet articles, and other gear in the suitcases. He had bought two because he wanted to keep his walking gear, knapsack, blanket and other things for the trek down to Hoa Da, which he hoped would not be too far in the future.

The desk clerk told him the bus for Dalat would leave at three o'clock, so Lyss checked out and made his way to the hotel that also served as a bus depot.

The bus arrived and was not crowded. Lyss thought of the old days when people would be riding on the top, hanging onto the sides and baggage would be everywhere. It would appear, Lyss thought, that the new regime was successful with a good bus system, if this one was typical. It was orderly, appeared in good repair. When they left town the ride was comfortable. In about thirty minutes they descended to a small river and then began a steep climb. To the east Lyss could see one of the tallest mountains in South Vietnam. It was ruggedly beautiful country. The ravages of war seemed to have mostly disappeared. There was an occasional shell of a stone building, a house, or a business, usually on the edge of town where fighting had been more severe.

They set no speed records on the journey, arriving in Dalat about six o'clock. The bus stopped in front of the Majestic Hotel, which Lyss recalled was as good as the old Majestic in Saigon in times past. He was given a spacious room, descended to dinner and enjoyed a good rest for the night.

Next morning he walked slowly around the town, coming at last to the house he wanted to rent. It appeared the house was vacant, there being no signs of life or occupancy. It was the house Jim Shaw had occupied. The Bastille was easily visible only a block away. He felt incredibly lucky. He had entertained visions of having to bribe some people to vacate, which could have raised questions as to why he wanted that particular house so badly.

He then set out to find Vo Van Son, which turned out to be quite easy. Son maintained his headquarters only a block from the hotel. After thirty minutes, he was shown into a large office. Lyss had sent in his card.

"I have no need for construction at this time,

Mr. Farrar," the man behind the desk said.

"I have need of a nice home which I can use as my headquarters for the foreseeable future, Mr. Son," Lyss said. "General Tran Quoc Nha recommended I see you, not only for possible work, but he also said you might provide me with a house. I am particularly interested in one I saw this morning, which appears to be vacant. It is at number Twenty-four Mac Dinh Chi."

"Ah, but that is a very fine house, once owned by Nguyen Cao Ky. Our government has given me control, but there are few who could afford the price."

The expression on Son's face indicated he did not think a Filipino construction supervisor could rent such a house.

"What would the price be for a one year lease?" Lyss asked.

"The government approved price is one million, two hundred thousand dong."

That was about five hundred dollars a month, a real bargain. Lyss knew he would have to pay considerable under the table.

"That is very reasonable," Lyss said. "Surely that does not include the furnishings? Could you arrange to furnish the house for me? I will be glad to pay you well."

The talk, the dickering and the inuendoes went back and forth for better than an hour. The deal was sealed when Lyss produced ten Krugerrands, worth four thousand dollars in South Africa but worth twice that, if handled properly, in Vietnam.

Vo Van Son looked upon people in two categories, those who could be used or those who could be taken for money. He tended to judge others by his own standards. For example, he assumed any successful person in Vietnam had a private bank account in France, as he did. He had made a considerable amount of money in the sixties and the seventies, mostly by handling American cigarettes, clothing and arms on the black market.

Son had kept himself available to both the Thieu regime and the Viet Cong, but especially to the secret emissaries of General Giap of North Vietnam. He cultivated this relationship when it became obvious the Americans would leave and the South Vietnamese would be defeated.

Now he was what the old regime would call a provincial chief. The new regime merely called him the government representative. Son produced a bundle of keys, leaving Lyss to sort them out, except for the one to the front door.

"I will have my people clean the place and connect up the electricity tomorrow, so you may move in day after tomorrow. "When you are settled in, come back to see me. We will see what work arrangements we can develop. Construction is slow right now, but I expect it will brighten up a bit later."

Saturday Lyss found himself in the house he

had chosen in a conference halfway around the world. With help from Son, he found a couple to take care of the house and his kitchen.

He toured the house. As Jim Shaw had told him, he found it had a full basement. In Saigon, basements filled with water, but in the mountains of Dalat, they were practical. His first cursory look did not reveal the tunnel entrance. He postponed a detailed examination. He did not wish to show undue interest in the basement to his new servants. He was sure they were watching his every move with the natural curiosity of a new relationship. He must consider that the new servants were reporting on him to Son.

His first dealing with Son had confirmed what Jim Shaw had told Lyss in Virginia. Son was a slippery guy.

On Monday, he went to the bar of the Majestic for a relaxing drink. He suffered the second great surprise of his visit. At the bar, big as life, was Tran Van Thiet.

He had known Thiet in the days when he was one of the instructors at Vung Tau, the coastal resort town south of Saigon. The famous Major Nguyen Be was the Vietnamese commander at Vung Tau, where the provincial leaders of South Vietnam were trained under the auspices of the agency. They had even helped train the Phoenix teams, who would not have been so infamous if they had done what they were trained to do.

In the final days Thiet had escaped to America, so it was a double surprise to find him back in Vietnam under the new regime. He did not know whether to acknowledge him or not, so he waited for Thiet to take the lead.

Lyss sat at the bar and suddenly realized he had unconsciously made a mistake that could have been serious. Of course Thiet would not take the lead, you stupid worm, Lyss said to himself. He does not know Juan Farrar.

He went over to the bar stool where Thiet sat and spoke, in Vietnamese, at an appropriate moment.

"Aren't you Tran Van Thiet?"

When Thiet looked up to him with a smile, Lyss said, "I am Juan Farrar. I work for Occidental Construction. We are trying to get business going here again."

"Yes, I am Thiet. I have come back to be with my countrymen. I am doing some work with the police here. Where did you know of me?"

"In Vung Tau. Where is Major Be now?"

"He went to America and has remained there. I hear he is not in the best of health."

"I am living at Twenty-four Mac Dinh Chi. I would be most pleased if you would have dinner with me there tonight."

Lyss waited a moment, and then said, "Or another day if it is better for your schedule. We could talk about the war days, but more importantly, you might help me with my current program."

"It would be a pleasure. Is eight o'clock satisfactory?" Thiet said. There seemed to be a smile on his face.

"Eight o'clock is fine. I will see you then."

Lyss hastened back to his home to alert his cook, who in a few hours would put a meal on the table. Lyss hoped it would be a good one.

It was just a few minutes after eight when Thiet arrived and immediately spoke to Lyss in English.

"It is good to see you again."

English was a common language of the Philippines, Lyss thought, but he felt there might be more to it than that. During the dinner of lobster and shrimp, they talked in both English and Vietnamese.

After dinner, Lyss brought out a bottle of cognac and poured liberal helpings into two snifters.

"There was an American I knew fairly well in Vung Tau," Thiet said after a quiet period.

"He did not live there, but came to see Major Be rather often. I dined at his table once in Saigon. There is something about you, a Filipino, which reminds me of Colonel McCutcheon, the American. I liked him, what I saw of him, so I am prepared to like you and to be your friend."

Lyss was in a turmoil. He maintained a calm exterior. Obviously, Thiet was giving an open invitation. Lyss decided he must be very careful. Instinctively, he felt Thiet was one of those Vietnamese who had worked with Americans who could still be trusted. But he wanted to examine the situation closer before accepting this invitation.

"I am flattered. Not all Americans are worthy of such memories, nor Filipinos, nor Vietnamese. McCutcheon must have been an honest man.

"Why did you leave America to return to Vietnam?"

"I think it was for two reasons," Thiet said. "First, I am Vietnamese, this is my homeland. I missed it too much.   Second, I thought I might serve my own country in its time of need. It has not been easy.

"I have been through reindoctrination, which is nothing for men of average intelligence. I believe Vietnam can again be a country for the free and the understanding. It has never been a true democracy and probably never will be, but, at least, it can be a benevolent government run by the elite without necessarily bending our knee to Karl Marx."

"What would happen to you if some of the leaders of the new regime heard you talking like that?" Lyss asked.

"It would depend largely on who it was. If it was General Nha in Ban Me Thuot, he would probably agree with me. If it was Son here in Dalat, he might recommend me for more reindoctrination. Son always plays the winning side of the street. I do not trust him.

I suggest you be on your guard.

"I feel sure you are not here to build. But whatever you are here for, do not trust Son. It is enough that you have rented one of his houses."

"Thank you for your candor," Lyss said. "What you have said is safe with me. We shall see more of each other, much more, I hope."

Shortly, Thiet left the house. Lyss thought about the unusual evening and the forthrightness of his guest. As with General Nha, Thiet had probably had some inner feeling that may have been a break in Lyss's disguise.

Yes, he thought, we should have changed the voice.

Lyss sat down to contemplate this second surprise. He pondered the effect upon his mission. He concluded the overall effect was probably good. He could count on Thiet to help him in Dalat. For this reason he decided to brief Thiet on his mission, omitting some details.

It had been a dreary, rainy day in Dalat, a common occurrence in this mountain town. Lyss decided, even in the dark and threatening night, to go for a walk and do some thinking. He slipped on a jacket and stepped out into the cold, wet air.

As he cleared the gate and turned right, he felt a heavy hand slap him at about the level of his money belt and then a sharp pain in the right side.

Instantly, he drew out the Air Force knife from

his belt buckle and swiftly spun, slashing with the sharp edge. He caught the assailant in the edge of the throat. He brought his hand, and the knife, back to the left, and slashed again. Blood spurted from a cut jugular. The man collapsed on the sidewalk.

Lyss knew he was bleeding from his right side. He had not yet begun to feel the effects, so he stepped quickly back into his house. He sat heavily on the big sofa, removed his money belt and hastily stuffed it under the sofa cushion. Unless Vietnamese police had changed in the past few years, Lyss felt he should not have the money belt on, especially if he was to be taken either to the police station or the hospital.

Then he called to Cuc, his housekeeper. She came into the room promptly.

"Get the police and a doctor, Cuc, and hurry."

She called her husband who left immediately. Cuc then asked Lyss to lie face down on the couch. She ripped his shirt to expose the wound.

He began to feel the pain of the wound and moaned a bit, then asked Cuc if she could tell much about the nature of the cut.

"No," she said. "It is a small wound like a stiletto. It is just above your belt line."

"Just put a compress of some kind on the wound and bind it until the doctor gets here," Lyss said.

Cuc left to get hot water and towels, returned quickly, and washed the wound, which was not bleeding very much.

"It looks like it was a thin, sharp knife," she said. "The question is how deep it has gone. Are you having any difficulty breathing?"

"No," Lyss said. I think it is too low for the lung, but I hope it has not penetrated the liver."

Shortly a policeman came.

He announced the man on the sidewalk was dead. He had been previously caught in a robbery.

"Good riddance, and I think the magistrate will agree. How badly are you hurt?"

"I don't know," Lyss said. "It's very painful. I hope the liver hasn't been damaged. We will leave the decision to the doctor."

"There is little chance of getting a doctor at this hour. Let me take you to the hospital."

Cuc's husband returned to say no doctor was available.

Lyss let the policeman take him to the hospital, which was small but clean.

Turning to the policeman, Lyss said, "My thanks to you for your help. Could I ask a favor? At dinner tonight my guest was Tran Van Thiet. I understand he works with you police. Could you let him know I'm here?"

"Certainly. Mr. Thiet is a good man."

Within two hours or so Thiet arrived. The

doctor still had not seen Lyss.

"After you left," Lyss said, "I was thinking a great deal and decided to take a walk. I was attacked. We will not know how bad I am cut for a while. The police tell me I killed him. They seem happy about it."

"Yes," said Thiet. "He was a known criminal who had stayed a jump or two ahead of us. He jumped one too many, didn't he?"

"A man must learn to defend himself," Lyss said. "I have taught myself how to use both a knife and a gun. Thinking over our talks this evening, I have decided to place my complete trust in you.

"It will require one special task of you as soon as you can. I was wearing a money belt, which, no doubt, was what the robber was after. Although I have no idea how he knew I had a money belt. It is now under the sofa cushion in my living room. I would appreciate it if you would get it and keep it safely for me until I get out of here."

"If in dealing with Son you exposed the fact that you have a money belt, it gives me an idea where the robber got his lead," Thiet said with a twinge of bitterness in his voice.

"That robber is the typical hoodlum available for hire. I have a strong feeling about who hired him."

"Yes," Lyss said. "There was some money given under the table to get the house. I did excuse myself and go to the bathroom to get some gold from the money belt. It is entirely possible he assumed I had a money belt and that was the reason I went to the bathroom."

Thiet's face was strained with worry, as he said, "Take care, Juan, take care!"

DRAGONS YET TO SLAY

CHAPTER FIFTEEN

It was mid-morning before the doctor saw Lyss. The wound was closed. His side and back were no longer in pain. Also by that time, Thiet had come by to say everything was safe, and he would drop by in the afternoon for a visit.

The doctor said from the position of the wound, his only fear was damage to the right kidney. A check of his urine showed no blood, so the doctor gave him a tetanus shot and some pills. He told him he could rest and heal at home as successfully as in the hospital. He invited Lyss to come back to see him if any problems developed.

At mid-afternoon Thiet went to the hospital and found that Lyss had been sent home. He went to the secure place, retrieved the money belt and went to Lyss's house. He was propped up in bed, notebook in his hand and a wide smile on his face. Thiet handed Lyss his money belt.

Lyss pondered the problem of Thiet, feeling sure Thiet was well aware Lyss was in country for something secret. The plan discussed in Virginia had included getting help from Vietnamese, if Lyss could find one he could count on. Lyss felt Thiet was one worthy of his trust.

Lyss turned to Thiet and said, "My friend, I have placed my money in your hands. Now I will place my life in your hands as well. My task here is to rescue a good man from imprisonment and get him out of the country. It is a complicated affair. I will keep you informed as it goes along.

"I need your help. Right now I need several hundred cement building blocks, as nearly as possible like those you will find in the basement of this house. I need some cement and sand so I can put those blocks together in a wall I will build in the basement. I would prefer no one know that I am working with building material, but it may be impossible to hide. I will also need about a gallon of muriatic acid.

"It will be several days before I can do that kind of work, but thank God I heal quickly. This is a setback no one counted on. Can you help me? Will you help me?"

"Yes, I will help you, but you must understand there are some limitations to how much I can help you. Your building blocks and cement are no problem. I am doing some work with the police, so I do not want to know the details of your attempt at what you call a rescue. Later, when you succeed, it might be difficult for me if I had something to do with a jailbreak."

"I understand. I'll protect you in every way I

can. Further, if I ask something of you that will endanger yourself, do me the favor of refusing."

"The building material will be here in three days. I may not accompany it. There's a man I trust to deliver the material to you for the partition in your basement. I think I should not be seen here too often, so I'll visit with you mostly at night."

Lyss fretted at the time it took for his wound to heal with pain hitting him in the back if he tried any normal exercise. When called to the magistrate for the hearing, he went, careful not to use his back muscle. Lyss was exonerated. The hearing proceeded in a routine fashion until the magistrate asked to see the knife Lyss had used to defend himself.

"One of my American Air Force friends gave it to me while I was working on a job at Clark Air Force Base."

He pulled the knife from its belt buckle holster and handed it to the magistrate.

"Very clever," the magistrate said, "and obviously very useful."

When Lyss returned home, he asked Cuc to get him a pick and a shovel.

"I want to dig in the yard."

Jim Shaw had been clever in closing up the entrance to the tunnel. He had told Lyss they sealed it up just before they evacuated the house.

Lyss finally found it and began the laborious

task of removing the cement blocks. He built a partition to make a small room that enclosed the tunnel entrance. The only entrance into the secret room from the main basement was through a closet with a removable back panel.

He washed the new wall seams with muriatic acid. When he finished all walls looked the same. He stood back, like an artist admiring a new painting. He was thankful that in West Virginia he had helped Gordon Shaffer remodel a cement block room. Gordon had used the same acid treatment to make the mortar seams in the wall look alike, whether old or new.

If he had to hide Harvey away here in the house, he now had a small room that would be difficult, if not impossible, for an uninformed person to find.

He would have liked to have a West Virginia coal miner's lamp, but he had to get by with a kerosene lantern and candles. All the houses in Vietnam had candles for use during the frequent power outages.

The tunnel was open all the way, although some dirt and debris had fallen to the floor. The southern entrance, which Jim had told him was in the edge of the mountain, was firmly closed with rock and cement. He decided to leave it closed for the time being.

There were the expected cobwebs and spiders and assorted other insects, but Lyss was pleased to find the tunnel in relatively good shape. Even as a boy, Lyss had not liked spiders. He wished he had some spray to clear the tunnel.

DRAGONS YET TO SLAY

He did not know if they were poisonous or not, but adopted the attitude of leave them alone and hope they would leave him alone.

Lyss marveled at the amount of work originally done to dig the tunnel. He confirmed Jim's measurement of two hundred and fifty yards long.

In getting the door open from the basement into the tunnel, Lyss had broken some cement blocks. Gathering some of the larger of the broken pieces, he carried them into the tunnel to use as markers.

He used his own paces as a measuring tool. He placed the first good marker at a hundred paces, then one at a hundred and thirty, which he estimated to be the center of the Bastille's north side.

Outside, as though he was taking an afternoon stroll, he paced from the edge of the house along the north wall of the Bastille. He carefully recorded the paces to the northeast corner and from the house. This confirmed the estimate he had made in the tunnel.

It now was time to locate Harvey.

He returned to the office of Vo Van Son, the first time he had seem him since Lyss's accident. Lyss tried to talk in the same manner as he had in past meetings with Son, but it was difficult to conceal his dislike and distrust of the man.

"Ah, Mr. Farrar, it is good to see you were not seriously hurt. I would have called on you, but I have been out of town. I was called to Ho Chi Minh City.

"Can I be of any help to you today?"

"Yes, if you can give me some information," Lyss said. Before I left Manila, the family of a Filipino called on me to see if I could locate the head of the family, one Jose Mendoza. I do not know him, but they said he was in prison in Dalat. Can you help me find him?"

"I have never heard of him," Son said, "but I will inquire and see what I can find out.

"You say you do not know this Mendoza?"

"That is correct, but I agreed to see if I could do anything for a fellow Filipino."

As he left, Lyss felt sure that Son was lying. In his position of responsibility, he would certainly know about foreigners who were incarcerated.

He was delighted when Thiet came to the house after dinner that night. He posed the same problem to him.

Thiet said Mendoza was probably in the Bastille. It would be difficult to get to see him.

"Thiet, My friend," Lyss said, "I want to assure you Mendoza is not the person I seek to rescue. I'm merely trying to help out a fellow Filipino, and, therefore, I'd like to see him. I tell you this as a part of our agreement not to involve you in the intimate details of my misssion here."

"Then if you can be above board about it," Thiet said, "I simply would go to the police chief and pose your problem directly with him.

"I agree with you that Son is lying. There's little you can do about it. There's a possiblity I can help you locate this Mendoza, but I think you should go to the police chief first."

Lyss had to wait thirty minutes to get in to see the police chief. Thirty minutes appeared to be the standard heel cooling time under the new regime, although he had to wait an hour to get in to see General Nha the first time in Ban Me Thuot. Waiting rooms were made to impress visitors with the importance of the man upon whom they were calling.

"The family of Jose Mendoza," Lyss said, "a Filipino whom I do not know, asked that I seek to find him, and perhaps take some extra food or cigarettes to him. They said the last word they had was that he was in prison in Dalat. Would it be permissible for me to see him?"

"I will have our records checked and see if such a person is in our custody and if visitation is possible," the chief said.

"Please come back tomorrow and see me."

Lyss thought Asiatic and American bureaucrecy had several things in common, not the least of which was to consume as much time as possible.

Feeling confident things were progressing satisfactorily, he returned home and walked the tunnel again. He saw fewer spiders this time. He surmised they had moved to the farther reaches of the passage. Consulting his figures he reaffirmed his earlier conclusion that the center of the Bastille was close to a hundred and thirty paces from the house basement entrance. He planned a new tunnel, at right angles to the old one, directly to the Bastille wall. If his calculations were right, the new passage would reach the prison wall about at the partition between cells three and four.

Lyss went over his thought processes. He had a hunch that Harvey was in one of the center cells, either three or four. Lyss always played his hunches, but he also felt that an important prisoner would be kept in sight as much as possible. Center cells would provide the guards with their best view.

Further, Jim had said there were six cells of equal size, and that would put the wall between cells three and four in the center of the building.

Lyss began his new tunnel toward the huge building. He found the digging easy in places and difficult in others. He believed there was four feet of dirt and rock above the four-foot ceiling. This gave him confidence that noise of digging was not one of his problems.

He dug only about an hour at a time, resting in between. It was during some of these rest periods that he decided to furnish the secret room. Again, he had an overwhelming feeling he would need this room for Harvey, certainly for days, and perhaps for weeks.

He returned to the police chief and received exactly what he had expected. The chief said there was no record of any Mendoza, much less a Jose Mendoza.

DRAGONS YET TO SLAY

When Thiet came to visit the next night, he told Thiet of his roadblock and asked for suggestions.

"I may be skating on thin ice," said Thiet, "but I think I have an idea."

It was only two days later that he was surprised to see Thiet at the front door in the middle of the afternoon.

"I'm here officially to advise you the file on Jose Mendoza has been found. You may visit him at three o'clock tomorrow afternoon."

When they got into the house, Thiet told Lyss he had searched more carefully kept files. He had found the Mendoza file and had reported it to the chief of police.

Thiet said the chief was not happy to have the file found. Thiet had handed it to him in the presence of some other officers. The chief had no choice but to acknowledge it and direct Thiet to make the arrangements for Mr. Farrar.

"So, my friend Juan," Thiet said with a smile, "tomorrow you may look inside the Bastille. Since I'm officially assigned to the case, I'll accompany you. I believe we can walk to it from here." He laughed.

"I searched my mind to determine why both Son and the police chief were reluctant to have you visit with Mendoza. I concluded they do not want you, or any other foreigner, to see the American who is in cell four.

"Adding this to what you have told me confidentially, my curiosity immediately brought the question to my mind as to whether this American is the man you are really seeking or not, but I'm not going to ask you about it. I'm saying to you that you must be very careful.

"I have great admiration for this American, because he has told his interrogators nothing, and he does not complain. Perhaps you'll see for yourself tomorrow, but if he's the object of your search, please do not tell me. I don't want to know."

Lyss was somewhat taken aback by this conversation. He got the feeling Thiet really hoped the American was the object of Lyss's announced rescue effort.

After Thiet left Lyss put on his jumpsuit and immediately went to work on the passage. Thiet's announcement that the American was in cell four substantiated his plans for running the tunnel to the center of the north wall.

He found himself digging almost frantically. Then he stopped and told himself to take the necessary time, move carefully and be thorough in every task before him.

DRAGONS YET TO SLAY

CHAPTER SIXTEEN

Lyss awoke early the next morning. He was as anxious as a young boy to get into action. This could be the beginning of the success of his tasks. It did not occur to him it could also be the beginning of failure.

He fidgeted around in the morning, rehearsing his plan and nibbling at the food Cuc put in front of him. He paced the floor, worked over the Morse code he was planning and imagined the results of the day.

Lyss assured himself he was a practical man, not given to fantasies, but he found himself acting like a schoolboy on his first date. He knew he must calm down.

By the time Thiet came, just before three o'clock, Lyss was settled into a more placid, more controlled mien.

"I thank you for coming, Thiet. Perhaps we can help one of our fellow men."

They walked the few yards to the entrance of the Bastille. Lyss admired the massive stone building with its recesses in the walls to make the corners appear as broad columns. The French had deliberately designed their *casernes* and their prisons to appear impregnable.

They registered at the desk in the lobby of the building and were escorted down to the basement.

Jim's description of the north area was accurate. With a quick glance at the center cells, he spotted Harvey and was appalled at Harvey's obviously bad condition. He looked away to the Filipino, who had been brought from his cell to a table where Lyss sat opposite him.

If the cells were numbered from the front of the building, Harvey was in number four. Lyss must handle his visit with Jose Mendoza as an obvious priority.

"Your family asked me to see if I could find you and to see if there was anything I could do to make you comfortable," Lyss said. He spoke in Tagalog. The guard immediately spoke up and demanded they speak only in Vietnamese.

Lyss was faced half toward Harvey and turned his head a bit. In years past, Harvey and Lyss and other Morse code students had often teased guests at parties by speaking in Morse code with their eyes.

Lyss wiped his hand across his eyes and blinked the code for L Y S S. He looked away at Mendoza.

"I thank you very much. How is my family?" Mendoza said.

"They told me to assure you they are well, but

they miss you," Lyss said. Lyss passed him a carton of American cigarettes.

"They told me if I gave you these Marlboros, you would know I spoke for them."

He looked back at Harvey, who blinked A K for acknowledged.

"What can I do for you, Senor Mendoza," Lyss asked in English.

The guard pounded on the table.

"Speak Vietnamese."

"Nothing," Mendoza replied. "My stay here is in the hands of the gods. I will survive. Perhaps you can come back to see me occasionally?"

"I would hope so," Lyss said, again wiping his eyes. He blinked, half looking at Harvey, N O R T H.

He took out his handkerchief and wiped his eyes.

"I am having trouble with my eyes."

Then he blinked W A L L.

Again Harvey blinked back A K.

As far as Lyss was concerned, his mission was now accomplished. So he visited a bit more, wiping his eyes occasionally, then told Mendoza he would be back in three days.

"What can I bring you? Some food?"

Mendoza declined.

"You will not believe it, but the food here is

quite good. At least for me. I know the American in cell four is given very little food. There is no way I can share mine with him."

As Thiet and Lyss reached the guard in the lobby upstairs, Lyss turned to the guard and said, "I promised him I would be back in three days. Is a special permit required?"

"No, you have been granted permission to visit the prisoner. It is customary to permit two visits a week."

Upon return to his home, Lyss invited Thiet in for a drink which he accepted. As they sipped wine, Lyss thanked him for his help.

"I don't see why both Son and the chief didn't want to admit Mendoza was in prison, but you are probably right. They didn't want me to see the American," Lyss said.

"That American is a good man," Thiet said. "He has resisted interrogation and gained the admiration of almost every man who has worked on him. He will talk about clouds and sky and sea, but nothing about the military or intelligence."

"Some Americans can be stubborn," Lyss said.

"To you, and you only, I'll say I wish they had been more stubborn in fighting a war," Thiet said wryly. He shrugged his shoulders.

"We must face today and not live in yesterday.

"Thank you for the drink. Let me know when you want to see Mendoza again."

He left.

Lyss hastily changed into one of his jumpsuits.

Harvey's condition was an obvious warning that time could not be wasted. Anyway, Lyss was anxious to dig. He went into the tunnel. He believed he had about reached the outer wall area. He did not know whether he would strike foundation or stone. Actually, he hit neither. The ground became softer. He had to beware of a collapse of the ceiling of his new tunnel.

As he reached the wall, about an hour after he started the evening's digging, the loose ceiling fell. He saw the cement of the foundation of the outer wall.

Reluctantly he stopped and returned to the house. He knew he must be patient. Having seen Harvey he also knew it was imperative he rescue Harvey as soom as possible.

He washed and put on clean clothes in time to respond to Cuc's call for dinner. It was an excellent meal. He had not eaten well all day, so he really enjoyed it.

Lyss sat in the living room with a book until Cuc came in to tell him good night. Then he went to his room and donned his work clothes again.

There was a small garden cart he had smuggled into the tunnel, using it to spread the dirt in even piles along the outer part of the main tunnel. It took him quite a while to clean up the excess from the afternoon fall below the foundation of the outer wall.

Examining that foundation, he developed an idea on closing off the tunnel. He dug about a foot wider on each side of his tunnel, even with the wall. Later, he hoped to have time to fill up all the tunnel from the outer wall foundation to the Bastille. He planned to build his own wall beneath the foundation to enclose the area between the outer wall and the Bastille.

He decided to slope the tunnel downward as he dug toward the basement wall. Not only would this assure him of reaching the level of the floor of Harvey's cell, but it would also facilitate the filling in after Harvey had been removed. He kept to the basic dimensions, three feet wide, four feet high.

The softer soil was easier to dig, but more dangerous. *I really ought to get some timbers in here and shore up that ceiling.*

Almost as soon as the thought occurred to him, he suddenly felt dirt hitting him in the back. A pile of earth tumbled onto him. He had the presence of mind to brace himself and hold up off the floor with his arms, but the pressure was heavy. He had an air pocket under him and kept himself as calm as possible. He deliberately slowed down his breathing.

Lyss could move his legs, so he knew the pressure was only on his body. Slowly, he began to inch his way back. If the whole ceiling had collapsed up to ground level, he was done for, both literally and in his tunnel plan.

If the collapse had exposed his digging to the

surface above, he was in deep trouble.

Little by little he inched his way back. Finally the way became easier, and he was clear. He took several deep breaths and was pleased to find he was none the worse for the accident.

He quickly examined the tunnel and found less than two feet of the ceiling had fallen on him. He knew if it had been much more he would have been buried alive. His whole project would have been ended.

He ceased work for the night, planning on getting some lumber into place the next morning.

Lyss went into the backyard, took off his jumpsuit and shook it out thoroughly. He returned to his room for a bath and bed.

He received another shock at breakfast.

Cuc served his breakfast, then respectfully waited for Lyss to invite her to speak.

"Monsieur Farrar," she said, speaking in French.

It was the first time she had ever spoken French with Lyss. They had always conversed in Vietnamese.

"My husband and I want to be of greater service to you, and we believe we can. We must trust you with our secret. We worked in this house years ago for Monsieur Jim Shaw."

She pronounced it Zheem.

"Monsieur Jim was a fine man, gentle and kind. In our own limited way, we helped him dig the tunnel in which you are now working. We do not know your purpose, but we feel it is right and proper for us to help you, whatever your plan. Will you trust us?"

Lyss was startled and speechless.

"Let me think a moment," he said in French.

He casually sipped on his coffee, touched some egg with a fork, then looked up.

"Would you object to telling me a bit of your life's story?"

"Not at all," Cuc said. "We are trusting you. We must continue to trust you in every way. We did not have the same names when we worked for Monsieur Jim. After the Americans left, we hid out for a while. Later we came back into life with our present names. There is no record that we had worked for Americans.

"It was difficult, but we managed to eat. Then we met Mr. Son, who gave us some work to do. We have been house servants for many years. My husband is a very good cook. He was trained years ago by the French in Hanoi."

"After the great battle of Dien Binh Phu, we were given the opportunity to move into the south. We came to Saigon. Not too long after that, we came to Dalat and found work with an American in this house. Later Monsieur Jim came here. We were very happy. We trust we served him to his satisfaction.

"When the great battles of Tet took place, we had gone to our homes for the holidays. We came back as soon as we could to help Monsieur Jim. After the battle was won, Monsieur Jim started digging the tunnel. We offered to help. He let us do a little bit as he directed us. We knew it was an escape route in case of further trouble.

"When Mr. Son asked us to work here for you the other day, we were delighted. We love this house, but we hope for a new future some day."

Lyss remained quiet for several minutes. Cuc stood by, patiently waiting.

Lyss made his decision. He had said in the early briefings that perhaps some of the people who had helped in the past would be found and would give assistance. He decided to risk telling Cuc and Duong of his mission and to solicit their help.

"First, I thank you for your offer. It may be dangerous for you to help me. I will make every effort to protect you.

"You have served me dinner in years past. I was here only once, briefly, after Tet. I thought there was something familiar about you and certainly Duong's good cooking. Your name was not Cuc and Duong then and mine was not Juan Farrar. It is just as well that we not pursue the question of names.

"A friend of mine is a prisoner in the Bastille, as we call it. It is my mission to rescue him and take him out of Vietnam. The prisoner was also one of Monsieur Jim's friends. That is why I am digging in the tunnel and why I have added a secret room to the basement."

Cuc did not change expression during this revelation, but she had smiled when Lyss said the prisoner was one of Monsieur Jim's friends.

"There's much to be done. Time is important because my friend in prison is in very poor health. When I get him out, he may need some time here to recover. That is why I built the special room, which, obviously, was not kept secret from you.

"Now, I have an urgent need for some heavy timber to shore up the new part of the tunnel. Part of it caved in on me yesterday. I would like for Duong to get me some timbers and some big nails. Do you think he can get such material for me?"

Cuc nodded and left.

DRAGONS YET TO SLAY

CHAPTER SEVENTEEN

Following Lyss's instructions, Cuc's husband, Ly Van Duong, brought a cartload of two-by-six, rough lumber and several pounds of heavy nails. They carried the wood into the basement. Lyss began sawing it into three and four-foot lengths. Then he nailed them together and carried them into the tunnel.

Duong helped with the carrying. It was the first time any other person had seen his newly dug tunnel.

Lyss had accepted the offer of help from Cuc and Duong because he believed the story Cuc had told him. It fitted into his prior knowledge of Jim Shaw and his ability to make really good friends. Having seen Harvey and his condition, he knew time was important. Recognizing the risk, he decided to use their help, hoping he could protect them from possible repercussions from Son and others.

With Duong hauling dirt with the cart, the digging became faster. Lyss shored up the tunnel as he went. He reached the stone wall of the Bastille in two days. The stones were of medium size, obviously carefully hewn. Making as little noise as possible, Lyss bored a half inch hole through the mortar at a corner of four stones, approximately, he hoped, a foot above the floor inside and behind Harvey's bed.

He tried to look through the hole, but something was obstructing the view. He hoped it was Harvey's bed.

The next day was the time for him to again to visit Jose Mendoza. He checked with Thiet, who said he would not need an escort. All he had to do was show up at two o'clock and the guards would let him visit with Mendoza.

He had managed to find a small box of chocolates, so he wrapped that as a gift for Jose. He prepared a Band-Aid message for Harvey in case he had a chance to give it to him.

The guards did not seem pleased to see him, although he gave each a package of cigarettes. After a small delay, they escorted him to the basement. Jose was at the table waiting for him. Before he seated himself, he walked to Harvey's cell and said, "They will not let me bring you food, but I brought a bandage for your injured finger."

"Thank you," Harvey said.

The guard hastened to Lyss and pulled him away by the arm. "This prisoner must not be spoken to."

Lyss turned and said, "I merely gave him a bandage for his finger."

He saw Harvey tear the backing off the Band-Aid, place the bandage around his finger and stuff into his pocket the backing on which Lyss had written a message:

What time tonight can I talk to you through the hole?

Lyss turned to Jose and gave him the box of chocolates. He told him he had written to his family two days earlier, but no one could tell him when the letter might get to Manila.

"Even from two towns in the Philippines, it is difficult to know when a letter will be delivered, as you know, Senor Farrar," Jose said after thanking him for the candy.

Harvey had sat down on his bed. Lyss noted he had carefully removed the bandage backing from his pocket. He proceeded to place them in his mouth and chew on them to obliterate the writing. Then Harvey swallowed the bandage backing.

While talking to Jose, Lyss looked toward Harvey and Harvey's eyes blinked T E N.

Harvey's face was still drawn with bruises. The right hand was swollen and blue.

After visiting a while with Jose, Lyss turned toward Harvey and blinked A K.

Saying his farewells to Jose, he promised to return in four days. Jose had no special requests of him.

Upon his return to the house, Lyss realized he had two equipment needs. He needed a block and tackle and some sort of tongs which would fit over an eighteen inch stone. He shopped carefully, spotting the block and tackle in one store. He had to go to a bricklayer to find tongs that would serve his purpose. He bought a set of tongs, but asked Duong to go to the store and get the block and tackle.

Lyss read a little while, trying to rest. Then he enjoyed a good dinner.

He could not refrain from going into the tunnel. He had placed his tools in the proper position and had driven a strong stake into the ground. He would base his block and tackle there, and use it to pull the stones from their places when the time came.

First, he must know which stones he was to clear. He could not know these until he talked to Harvey.

As he sat at the wall in the far end of the tunnel, he scratched at the mortar of the next stone west. He felt sure this would be one of the stones that would have to be removed.

It was slow and arduous work, taking out half inch thick mortar from around native stone, which, facing him, was about eighteen by eighteen inches. From the hole he had bored he knew the walls were two feet thick. So he knew the size of the stones he had to move. They were, he was sure, quite heavy.

He had made three tools from heavy knives to scrape the mortar from between the stones and had brought some three-eighths inch round rods on which to roll the stones as they came out. So he went to work on the vertical mortar crack eighteen inches west of his hole, feeling sure one or the other of the stones that touched the crack must be one of the two he knew he had to take out.

His plan was to remove the stones, pull Harvey through, then replace the stones as naturally as possible. He also had a plan to make it appear that Harvey had escaped out of his cell door. He hoped this would keep the guards from a close examination of the walls. He felt sure they would consider the walls impregnable and would look for other answers to Harvey's escape.

After two hours of exasperatingly slow work, Lyss suddenly realized the hour of ten was approaching.

"Can you hear me?"

He spoke slowly and distinctly.

"Naw, there's a buzzing in my ears."

"Cut the comedy, you bastard. I have to remove two stones. Which ones?"

"The next two west of this hole. They're behind my bunk."

"Is the guard alert?"

"No," Harvey said. "He's sound asleep and

across the big room. I knew he would be. That's why I chose ten o'clock."

"Then lie on your bunk a few minutes while I bore another hole, which should be at the top center of the two stones we will remove."

Lyss immediately went to work with the brace and masonry bit cutting a new half inch hole. In less than ten minutes he had the work done.

"Does that make much racket on your side, Harvey?"

"Very little. A while ago I could hear some scraping, but I doubt if the guard could hear it across the room even if he were alert."

"Let me have a few minutes. I'm going to pass a small penknife to you that may help. I'll stick the wire through, and you must be very gentle with it. Detach the knife and pass the wire back."

In a few more minutes, Lyss had pushed the wire through Harvey pulled it in carefully, taking the knife, then letting Lyss pull the wire back through.

"Next I'm sending a small ballpoint pen through to you," Lyss said. "Be careful with it. Josh Rosenbloom gave it to me. As it is, it'll write. If you hold down on the clip, while pushing down on the top, a needle appears. Another push on the top squirts a fluid through the needle. It'll knock a guy out for at least thirty minutes.

"My plan is for you to use it tomorrow night on your guard, take his keys, open your cell door, drop the keys and get back here and through the hole I'll have for you. Okay?"

"Gotcha. I'll keep the blanket down over the head of the bed, concealing the wall there. Don't do any work if you hear me talking loud," Harvey said.

"I think you can do a lot of work during the day, but don't get too deep in those mortar cracks until after ten o'clock tomorrow."

"I'm going to work on them tonight, so very little will need to be done tomorrow night. The tough job will be pulling those stones into my tunnel. Lie on your bed and keep your eyes and ears open while I work on this mortar."

After five hours of diligent work, Lyss had most of the mortar removed from each side of the two stones. He left what he estimated to be one inch on Harvey's side of the wall, planning on taking that out tomorrow. He braced the two stones with half inch steel rods. He placed his three-eighths steel rods under the stones. He made a pallet of strong wood on the floor of the tunnel, level with the bottom of the stones, then sloping up toward the main tunnel for a few feet.

"Harvey?" he asked through the hole.

"Yes."

"I'm stopping now. If all goes well, you'll be through here by midnight tomorrow."

"I am ready."

Lyss returned to his bedroom, bathed and went to bed. Even though it was four o'clock in the morning, and he had worked hard, he found it difficult to sleep.

Sleep finally came to him. He rested well until mid-morning. Cuc fed him an excellent breakfast. Lyss asked Cuc and Duong to meet with him after the meal.

"This will be a busy day and night," he said. "First, we need to prepare some broth for a man who has not eaten properly for more than two months. The bed in the secret room of the basement should be made ready.

"We'll need a stretcher so he can be taken to the bed.

"I suggest some rest this afternoon. A bowl of soup will do for my lunch, then an early supper.

"What we're about to do tonight is dangerous for us all. This is a critical time. I'll certainly understand if you wish to be relieved of your promise to help. You could take the day and tonight off and spend it with friends who can later vouch for your presence with them."

Lyss looked directly at Cuc.

"We did not idly make our promise," Cuc said. "We will be with you all the time. We'll do our best to be of service."

Turning to Duong, Lyss said, "We'll need thirty of the cement blocks near the entrance of the side tunnel and some water and mortar mix. I intend to wall the tunnel up underneath the prison fence as soon as the tunnel has served its purpose. Also, Duong, see if you can make asimple stretchen for the trip from the side tunnel to the bed.

"We'll need two shovels. Get as much rest as you can because tonight will be most demanding.

"Both of you have my deepest gratitude. The battle is not yet won, but, at least, we're beginning the campaign. Instead of the crossed sabers of the cavalry, we will use crossed shovels as our emblem."

CHAPTER EIGHTEEN

Vo Van Son sat at his desk in the government building pondering this Filipino who seemed only interested in the house Son had rented to him. Granted he had paid handsomely for the privilege, probably from a money belt filled with gold, but what was he really up to?

He sent out word to the police department to have Tran Van Thiet come see him. When Thiet arrived, Son said, "What do you know about this Juan Farrar?"

"Only that he seems to be what he says he is, a builder, or supervisor of builders, looking for money."

"When did you see him last?"

"Let's see," Thiet mused, privately wondering what this was all about.

"He came to me a few days ago in connection with visiting Jose Mendoza in prison. You had me escort him there last week for his first visit. I told him he didn't need an escort, as the guards now know him.

He visited there yesterday afternoon, taking a box of chocolates."

"I believe there is more to this man than meets the eye," Son said. "Keep me advised of what he does."

Lyss was finishing a late breakfast.

"Cuc, I will be in the basement for the next hour. I have a strong feeling we'll have a caller. Make him comfortable. Warn me so I may get here and be free of dirt when I see him."

Lyss puttered in the basement and the tunnel, smoothing out here and touching things there, like a nervous housekeeper expecting guests. He had the tools in place for the night's work when Cuc called him.

He hastily took off the jumpsuit and put on clean clothes, as well as cleaning up himself a bit, then presented himself in the living room.

Thiet was there in an uncharacteristic daylight visit.

"Son called me in this morning to ask about you," Thiet said. "I told him of your visits to Mendoza. He strongly suspects something, but does not know what. As a schemer himself, I think he's more provoked at not knowing what you're up to than whatever it is you are doing. He has asked me to report to him periodically about you."

"I see nothing wrong with his curiosity," Lyss said. "You can report to him that I'm disappointed the new regime hasn't yet come up with at least a building I can remodel for them. If we can keep him from any direct action for the next month, I think we'll be all right."

Thiet left. Lyss pondered this development. He dismissed it as unimportant and not worth worrying about, particularly on this day in which he had so much to do. He had no doubt the crafty Son could cause him a great deal of trouble, if he chose to. Lyss thought he would do a little work on Son, but later.

Harvey Zimmerman sat on the side of his bunk in his cell. He tried to look crestfallen, despite thoughts racing through him that in a few hours he might be free.

Harvey recalled that he and Lyss had not been friends. He did not agree with the way Lyss did some of his work. He really did not know whether Lyss could pull off this caper. However, it was evidence the agency had not forgotten him. They sent someone to get him out of this damned place.

Then he recalled how lucky Lyss had been. He privately hoped that luck would hold for one more job. The disguise amazed him, but he was happy to have recognized his voice.

Harvey would have put his head in his hands, but his hand was still swollen and blue in places, so he laid it in his lap. He made his plans for the evening.

His supper arrived, the usual piece of bread

and cup of water. They were keeping him alive. Harvey grimaced.

The interrogator delivering the supper was the same one who had been so brutal to Harvey. He had a crooked smile on his face.

As Harvey took his bread and water, he drained the cup and handed it back. He asked for more water. The interrogator brought a full cup. As Harvey reached for it, he threw it into Harvey's face and laughed.

He would have to find some way to get that bastard, Harvey thought. He went back to his bunk and lay down, careful to keep his head close to the hole in the wall.

Lyss was fretting away the time, thinking it would never be ten o'clock. He checked the pallet Duong had assembled and found it satisfactory. They placed it near the junction of the main passage and the tunnel toward the Bastille.

Duong put the building blocks into position. He put the mortar mix and water at one side. He had a small box in which to mix the mortar.

Lyss set up block and tackle and the tongs and finally, with a nervous twitch, pronounced everything ready.

He sat in the living room, having picked at a good supper, and finally Cuc brought him a scotch and water. He noticed she had been rather liberal with the scotch. He sipped it carefully. Lyss could not help but be a little nervous about the night's approaching work.

With the whiskey and some self control, he began to settle down a bit.

Finally, nine-thirty came. He and Duong went into the passageway prepared to get to work.

Lyss went to the hole a few minutes before ten and said, "Can you hear me, Harvey?"

"Yes."

"Is the guard asleep yet?"

"Yes."

"Are the two blocks concealed from your side?"

"Yes."

"Then I'll get busy. Don't do anything on your side until I tell you."

"Okay."

Lyss then went to work to clear the three vertical mortar lines, and then the bottom ones, holding the stones in place with the half inch rods. When he finished, he placed the three-eighths inch rods in place. With considerable effort, he withdrew the half inch rods.

Both stones slipped down slightly. He hooked the tongs onto one, then tied the block and tackle to it, stepped back, and started to pull.

The stone moved slightly. The rope stretched a bit. Suddenly the tongs slipped loose and flew back, hitting Lyss in the chest. He reeled back, gasping from the pain. He was sure ribs had been broken. When Duong rushed to him and blood began to stain the side of his jumpsuit, Lyss said, "No! No! Duong! We must keep at it."

He returned and refastened the tongs. He thought he had a better grip and again started to pull.

Slowly the stone rolled out on the three-eighths rods and finally rested three feet from the wall.

He quickly fastened the tongs to the other stone, which came out much easier and was soon beside the other.

"Okay, Harvey, get the guard to your door. Be sure he has his keys. When he gets there, get his arm through the bars and give him the hypo. Hang on because we need those keys."

"I'm on my way."

Lyss heard the door rattle and Harvey telling the guard the door was not properly fastened.

In less than a minute he heard a shuffling noise, a yell from the guard and then a sound like a body hitting the floor.

"Get over here, Harvey, and bring the keys."

He pulled Harvey through the wall. Harvey collapsed on the dirt floor of the tunnel. Lyss and Duong put him on the pallet. Duong started pulling him to the house.

"Get him in bed and let Cuc take care of him," Lyss said "Come back to help me."

Harvey had identified the guard as the one who had taken such joy in torturing him. Lyss crawled into the cell, took the keys and opened the door. The guard was sprawled on his back.

Lyss had killed before, but it was usually in self defense. This time he felt several factors required him to terminate this guard. One of them was the joy the guard took in torturing.

Lyss took out his stiletto, felt through the shirt for the third and fourth ribs and plunged the stiletto through his heart.

"That is for Harvey, you son of a bitch."

Very little blood came out with the knife. Lyss wiped the blade quickly, left the door ajar, turned back to the tunnel and began his reverse work.

He spread mortar carefully on the cell side of the hole, then added more to the top and sides of the first stone. Using the three-eighths rods, he slowly rolled the stone back into place. With his plastic tube, he squirted the mortar in every place after he had set the stone up on the half inch rods.

Duong saw what he was doing and said, "One moment. Let me get through the small hole and smooth the mortar of the stone that is in place."

"Thank God for small Vietnamese," Lyss said as Duong quickly did the job.

Then even more carefully, mortar was placed around the last stone. It was gingerly put in place.

Lyss thought it might show a bit, if they looked at it. With the door open, he was betting they would not look.

He took all the lumber out of the short tunnel, then began shoveling dirt back into the hole as fast as Duong could haul it to him. When he had the passage between the building and the wall foundation about half full, he started Duong hauling buckets of water which he threw into the dirt to help pack it down.

Then he built a concrete block wall under the outer wall foundation. When it reached up to within two feet, he left a hole about two feet wide.

He shoveled dirt into this area, occasionally pouring in water. Finally, it was practically full. He packed several more shovels full into the top and finished the wall.

Lyss felt if they at some future time did suspect the stones had been moved and removed them for a look, they would run straight into a blank wall of dirt.

It was four o'clock in the morning when they finished. They were exhausted.

Returning to Harvey's secret bedroom, they found him awake and sipping on chicken soup.

"I never knew chicken soup could taste so good," he said.

Then he turned to Lyss.

Tears came into his eyes as he reached out for Lyss's hand and tried to squeeze it.

"Thanks, Lyss."

Lyss pressed Harvey's hand and said, "This is

just the first inning, Harvey. We have a long way to go to win this ball game."

Lyss noted Duong and Cuc had left the room.

"We must leave you for a while, Harvey. When that guard is found, there'll be one hell of a hullabaloo. We'd better be prepared for the police to visit us. You have your water, and you have an old fashioned chamber pot, if you need it. Don't make a bunch of noise."

Lyss left, carefully securing the back of the closet which was the only door to Harvey's room.

He went straight to his bedroom and removed the jumpsuit he used as a work uniform. There was a patch of blood and sweat in the cloth of his left side. He went into the bathroom and bathed the area. He found he had a long abrasion, which had seeped blood but was now clotted over.

Taking a deep breath and feeling the pain, he knew he had bruised the muscles over the ribs and probably broken a rib.

There was nothing he could do about that but rest, breath deeply and wait. He had broken ribs before. While painful, he did not find them disabling.

He bathed, carefully applied antibiotic ointment to the abrasion, then covered it with a light bandage. He put on clean clothes. He then took the jumpsuit to Cuc and told her to launder it as soon as she could get to it. She handed him a cup of coffee and said breakfast would be ready shortly.

He sipped a bit of the coffee. Cuc brought in a plate of eggs and bacon. He knew Duong was as tired as he was. He appreciated the food.

Lyss looked at the calendar. It was April 26. Three days from the Hoa Da rendezvous. He knew Harvey could not travel, but he must make that meeting and give Al and Sarah a report.

DRAGONS YET TO SLAY

CHAPTER NINETEEN

Sarah Sanford could hear the hum of the silent outboard motor Alfred Bennett used as he was returning from placing Lyss on the beach at Ninh Hoa.

Sarah had never worried about the passage of time under emergency conditions, but she had fretted since it seemed to take so long for Al to get back to the *Pharaon*. He did return and smiled at Sarah.

"He's on the beach."

"Good," she said. "Are we going to wait a while?"

"We'll pull back several miles and wait twenty-four hours," Al said. "I told Lyss we'd be within signaling distance at ten o'clock tomorrow night."

The next night they came in and waited two hours. With no message they knew Lyss was on his way. They sailed out to sea.

"If you'll phrase the message, I'll send it to Manila," Al said.

Sarah replied:

The eagle has landed. Next contact on the twenty-ninth.

"Sarah, we have about eighteen days to wait. We could make it back to Manila in seven, stay there four days, then sail back here. Or we could do about the same by going to Singapore, although I'm reluctant to increase our communications distance.

"How would you like to take a walk on Hainan Island? We found a neat little coastal town, Yaihsein, on one of our cruises around. The area is unspoiled, both from a natural standpoint and a political one. The people had probably never seen an American until the day we landed. We suddenly had the urge. There was no real reason why we should land there. Even the one lone government official was friendly. We found one native who spoke French. My Chinese is pretty poor."

"That's strictly up to you, Al," Sarah said. "We must be sure to be back within signaling distance by the twenty-ninth."

The *Pharaon* sailed to the north in brisk winds. A few days later they put into the little shore town of Yaihsein. It was the first time Sarah had been in Communist China. Employees in her classification category were forbidden to enter either the Soviet Union or Communist China. If CIA headquarters knew about this visit, they would probably strongly disapprove. If they didn't know about it, they could not very well object.

There was a crude dock. Al hired a young man to watch the boat. Sarah wondered how much trust could be put in a young Chinese like that. Al replied they were too far from real civilization to be corrupted.

They walked around the clean little village and came to the small stone house where Al and Toni's friend lived. She welcomed them like long lost friends. She said there was no public restaurant in town and invited them to eat with her.

She served them some sweet and sour shrimp, white fish with the spicy Szechwan sauce and the inevitable rice. It pleased the hostess that they ate with chopsticks.

After four days, the visit began to wear on Sarah. Al suggested they start a leisurely trip back to the Hoa Da area.

"Let me show you the Paracel Islands, Sarah," he said laughing because the Paracels consisted of a group of unoccupied reefs. They sailed to the southeast to see this group of reefs. They saw no sign of life, but found a lovely coral beach the girls enjoyed immensely.

A few days later they were some fifteen miles off Hoa Da.

"Our contact time is ten o'clock the evening of the twenty ninth. Tomorrow is the twenty-eighth. I think we will go in after sunset to get within range. There's always a possibility Lyss has come early. If he spots us, he'll signal," Al said.

There was no response, even though they beamed a conventional message in Morse code toward the high hill north of the Hoa Da airstrip.

They pulled back and reentered the reception area the next night.

At ten o'clock they set the recorder on Lyss's frequency. Promptly there was a two second squirt message.

Al quickly replayed it at slow speed.

Harvey is out of prison. Secret place under my control.

Bad condition, will take two weeks to get him in shape to travel. Please return to this spot on May 12.

Acknowledge with A K by light only.

Al blinked A K toward the mountain, hoisted sail and left.

He turned the helm over to Toni and took Sarah below to their communications equipment.

"I don't like it, Al," Sarah said, "but we must do as he has asked. I'm afraid two more weeks might be too long for Lyss to live the life he's leading."

"Don't worry, Sarah. If he was having any trouble, he would have reported that, too."

Using voice transmission, he raised the Manila station. He transmitted a brief message saying all was well.

He reverted to the squirt at this point and transmitted Lyss's message. Then he transmitted several innocuous words about having a good time, but delayed two weeks.

To regular receivers the squirt message came through as a two-second beep.

Manila acknowledged:

Have good time. Will hear from you in two weeks.

All three of them were in the cockpit as they sailed away from the coast.

"Sarah, the weather forecasts are not good. This time of year we can nearly always expect a pretty bad storm. I would prefer to be south of our present location because I can count on prevailing winds to get us back here faster.

"The nearest port of shelter to the south of us is in the Kepulauan Islands. They are part of Indonesia, about four days away. The harbor at Netuna Besar is a good shelter. We could spend our dead week there with no problems but with nothing to do."

"You're the master of the ship," Sarah said with a smile. "You know this area of the world better than anyone. Besides, I think you have excellent judgment. Let's do what you think is best. Just so we are back at Hoa Da on May twelfth."

The three days leading up his transmittal to the *Pharaon* were busy, trying, and uncertain for Lyss.

The police, four of them, came to the house about 8:30 that morning, saying there had been an escape from prison and all houses in the area were being searched.

Lyss had anticipated this and had Cuc make extra coffee and put out some of Duong's fine pastries.

The search was thorough, including the basement, but they found nothing, enjoyed coffee and sweets and left.

Lyss dressed carefully and went to call on Son.

After the usual thirty minute wait, he was admitted.

"The police were at the house this morning and told me there had been an escape from the prison. I do not see how that could happen, Mr. Son, but I came to ask you if my friend Jose Mendoza was involved in any way."

"Apparently not at all, Mr. Farrar," Son said. "It was the American who made an amazing escape which we cannot believe. Somehow he got the guard to the door of his cell, killed him, and used the guard's keys to open the cell door. He simply disappeared. Mr. Mendoza was awakened by a scream from the guard. He thinks he saw the American go up the stairs soon thereafter. He says the light was dim."

"May I see Mr. Mendoza?" Lyss asked.

"Speak to the police about it."

Son almost grimaced.

"They probably will let you see him tomorrow, but I doubt if they want anyone in there today."

Lyss went to the police station and asked for Thiet, but he was not available. He asked to see the chief of police.

Again he had the usual thirty minute wait, but finally entered the chief's office.

"I do not wish to be a problem," Lyss said. "I would like to see my friend Jose Mendoza when it can be permitted. Mr. Son has told me he has been of some help to you in looking into the escape of the American. I would like to be able to assure his family in Manila that he is all right. In fact, if he agrees, we may seek a pardon for him so he can return to the Philippines."

"It is possible you can be of help to us, Mr. Farrar," the chief said.

"I will arrange for you to visit him this morning if you will ask him to tell you his story about last night and if you will come back and repeat it to me."

"I would be glad to," Lyss said.

The chief sent for another policeman, who then escorted Lyss to the Bastille and down to the cells.

Mendoza greeted him warmly.

"The American has escaped," he said. "I hope he gets away, but it is a mystery how he did it."

"I have come to ask your permission to intercede with the authorities and see if I can gain your release. I will probably have to assure them you will never return to Vietnam."

"If you can get me out," Mendoza said, "both my family and I will be forever in your debt. As for a return, I hope I never see this shitty place again."

"Now," Lyss said, "I have promised to get your story of what happened last night and relay it to the government officials."

"I have already told them all I know. I have told it to them without any reservation because it really is a remarkable thing. I heard the guard yell, then saw part of him as he lay on the floor. The light was dim, but I think I saw the American walking hurriedly up the stairs. I must have. How else could he have escaped? I just wish he had taken me with him."

"We will see what we can do," Lyss said. Then he turned to the guard.

"May I see the American's cell?"

"Yes," the guard said, "but do not touch anything."

Lyss then went into the cell, looked briefly and left. He was delighted there was no sign of any disturbance near the wall or near Harvey's bed.

He departed, went to the chief of police, and reported Mendoza's story was the same as he had told the police. Lyss added he believed he was telling the truth.

Lyss hastened back to his house because he had another task he must get done that day.

He found Harvey in good spirits and sitting up.

"You'll now see what a fine mason I am," Lyss said. He and Duong went to work to close up the opening into the tunnel area. It took Lyss most of the rest of the day. He again treated the wall with muriatic acid, as he had the previous construction. He was satisfied the entire wall looked uniform.

Then he headed back to Son's office, getting there late in the afternoon. He was only kept waiting about fifteen minutes.

"I have two things, Mr. Son," he said. "First, do you think it would be possible to get the magistrate to pardon my countryman, Jose Mendoza, if he promised never to return to Vietnam? If it could be settled with a fine, I would be glad to pay it."

Lyss clinked three gold coins in his hand as he talked.

"Perhaps," Son said. "I will look into it for you. It might be expensive, but I will do my best."

"Second, I have heard the docks at Phan Rang need some repair. I would like to go and see if I can get some work. Can you recommend a person I should see in Phan Rang? I think I will get a bicycle to go there. I have walked far enough."

"Yes," Son said. "I would recommend you see Nguyen Thien Duc, who handles the affairs to the town for the new regime. Why do you not hire a car for the trip?"

"It is a waste of money. I seem to have a great deal of time on my hands, so I will cycle down there in about six hours and be the healthier for it. Of course it will take me longer coming back because of the mountains."

Lyss left and found a good bicycle, which he bought. It was now late on the twenty-sixth, so he had an extra day. He planned to go to Phan Rang and spend two nights. He would cycle to near Hoa Da on the afternoon of the twenty-ninth.

He had no difficulty meeting this schedule. On the night of the twenty-ninth he climbed up a part of the mountain near the air strip at Hoa Da and sent his message. He was delighted with the quick flashlight response. He was back in Phan Rang by midnight and in Dalat by shortly after noon.

Lyss relaxed over a late lunch, then went to the basement for a visit with Harvey.

"Man, it surely isn't going to take many days of this chow to get me on my feet again," Harvey said.

"That's great," Lyss said. Then he told about his trip and his message.

"We'll now take nine days to get you into shape for a good walk. We'll head toward Saigon in a cart, with you concealed, until we reach a point I've selected. We'll then walk. I hope we can make it in two days, but I'll allow three. It is through fairly rugged country, but mostly downhill.

"If we get there a day early, we'll watch for the

ship. It is in character for Al to get to appointments early and case the joint when he can. Meanwhile, I have some cover work to do."

Next day, Lyss went to Son's office.

"Ah, good morning, Mr. Farrar," Son said.

"As I suspected, it will be rather expensive to get Mendoza released. If you can spare me ten of those gold coins, I think I can handle it. The fine levied is one million dong. I think if I use the gold in the right way, the ten coins will be sufficient."

"I will bring them to you. When can we get Mendoza released and given sufficient documents to leave via Ho Chi Minh City airport?"

"I will have him out this afternoon. There is a bus to Ho Chi Minh City tomorrow. I will arrange for documents."

"Good," Lyss said. "I will take him into my home tonight."

Lyss returned in less than an hour with the gold coins, including two extras he gave Son. He knew Son was probably pocketing some of the ten coin fine, but it was essential to keep Son happy.

"Can you arrange for Mr. Mendoza to be delivered to my custody now?" Lyss asked.

Son reached for the phone, spoke a few words, then turned to Lyss.

"Go straight to the prison. They will turn him over to you."

Lyss thanked him and left. Upon entering the prison first floor, he found Mendoza waiting for him with a small parcel of his effects.

Mendoza grasped his arm, then embraced him. Tears flowed from his eyes. His voice was unsteady as he spoke in Tagalog, "There is no way I can thank you, but if God gives me an opportunity, I will give him and you my best effort."

"We never know, Jose. We never know," Lyss said. He took Jose's arm and led him out the door and down the street to Lyss's house.

Together, they got some new clothes. They were almost the same size, so Lyss gave him one of his Philippine shirts.

Dinner that night was joyous. Lyss had thought of letting Jose see Harvey, but then decided there was nothing to be gained by it and a possibility of some loss. Harvey remained in seclusion until the next morning when Lyss took Jose to the hotel bus station and saw him depart.

DRAGONS YET TO SLAY

CHAPTER TWENTY

As the days went by Harvey's condition continued to improve so that Lyss had him come up to the dining room for his meals. He occasionally joined Lyss in the living room for a chat.

Lyss knew Harvey had regained sufficient strength and agility to enable him to get back to his hideaway quickly in case someone came to the house for a visit.

It was remarkable to watch Harvey's physical condition get better. Not only did he put on weight, but the exercises Lyss forced him to take improved his coordination and his attitude, although he protested loudly about assinine push-ups and knee bends. His wounds healed rapidly. Some burn marks remained, probably permanently.

It was on one of those cool, fresh evenings, after a steak dinner and several glasses of good wine, that Harvey told his story.

"They called me into the station in Bangkok and briefed me on Project Dragon. They asked me if

I would volunteer to locate and, if possible, define the installation the Soviets were putting into the Vietnam mountains.

"The early report was somewhat incomplete. They were installing a communications setup on top of one of the mountains. Our main concern was an unsubstantiated report it would include laser capasbility to down satellites and possibly intercept ICBMs. I never did understand why anybody thought they would set something up in this part of the world to shoot down intercontinental ballistic missiles. I still think that was Soviet disinformation.

"Anyway they briefed me right up to my keester. I memorized four likely locations, described in detail with aerial photos." Harvey chuckled.

"With a lot of imagination we named them Kruschev, Lenin, Stalin, and Trotsky.

"There's a mountain about eight thousand five hundred feet high north of Dak Gle. That was everybody's pick for Kruschev. Well, they dropped me on to the old Ho Chi Minh Trail across the border in Laos with plenty of gear and a good radio.

"I hiked it into Dak Gle, staying out of the village, but watching. You never saw a little thatched hut village so damned busy in your life. I spotted several Russians, not in uniform. One night I even got close enough to listen to them.

"My Russian never was much good, but I understood enough to know they had a big construction project on the mountain.

"I hauled ass to the mountain, found some fancy roads built up the side and the beginnings of construction. Incidentally, there was not the slightest evidence they were trying to hide what they were doing from aerial reconnaisance or satellite photos.

"I figured I'd found the site and it was Kruschev. I barreled ass down the mountain, went to my cache, got out the old radio and raised the Bangkok Station. I told them Site Kruschev was it, and I would keep digging."

Harvey stopped to sip on a glass of red wine and to catch his breath. His face took on a stern look as he continued.

"Well, they had documented me as a French geologist, just in case I surfaced somewhere. I decided to stray into Dak Gle and see if I could get anybody to talk to me.

"There was a new bar, well stocked with vodka and other necessities of life, so I went there and sipped on wine and listened. I couldn't seem to gather any real information, except I did hear one fellow talk about his headquarters being in Kontum, which was quite a ways away.

"So I hustle back to my cache to load up and start the hike south to Kontum.

"I stayed on the highway. I didn't see any reason not to. Before two days of walking had passed, some character in a car stopped and gave me a ride. It was wrong, but not as bad a mistake as I made shortly thereafter.

"He seemed like a pretty nice guy and told me he was working on the Dak Gle project.

"I should have smelled a rat, but I didn't. I asked some questions. By the time we got to Kontum he had decided I was a spy. He turned me over to the police.

"The Vietnamese police are better now than they used to be. They fingerprinted me and photographed me and put me in a solitary cell. In only a few days, one of the big shots came in to see me and addressed me as 'Harvey Zimmerman, American spy.'

"For reasons I've never understood, they moved me to Dalat and that shithole you found me in. During one of my interrogations, they let it slip they had turned my fingerprints and photo over to the Russians. It didn't take long for their file search to reap a harvest. And that, Lyss, shows you what a stupid ass you have rescued."

"Well," said Lyss, "let's see how soon we can get this stupid ass out of this country."

Lyss had discussed with Cuc and Duong his needs for the trip he had planned. They had agreed to find a farmer's cart with a vegetable load to be taken to Ho Chi Minh City for sale.

The next day, Duong returned with a well built cart and two oxen, all of which he put into the back yard. The cart was made of sturdy cuts of pine, with a solid floor six-by-six feet in size and with stanchions three inches square rising up five feet from the floor.

Lyss went to work on the cart, building a special bamboo laced enclosure. He made it two feet high, three feet wide and nearly six feet long. Then he immediately covered it with hay for feed for the oxen. At the appropriate time he intended to put a load of strawberries on top. This load was to be the reason for the trip to Ho Chi Minh City.

Lyss planned to leave within the next two days. They had finished lunch when Cuc asked to speak to him.

"Monsieur Juan," she said in French. "If we are to get Monsieur Harvey to someplace between here and Saigon, I think it best for you and Monsieur Harvey to dress like Vietnamese. I'll get the national black clothing and headdress. I believe you call them black pajamas and coolie hats. From a distance, you'll be less noticeable and at night almost invisible. Of course, if we are submitted to a close examination, it will be obvious that you are not Vietnamese."

"In that case," Lyss said, "I'll simply say I like the Vietnamese national dress and have adopted it for this rural trip. We'll keep Monsieur Harvey out of sight as much as possible, but the black clothing will help during those times we are stopped and he's out of his hiding place."

"We can arrange for the strawberries to be added to the cart at any time that suits your schedule," Cuc said. "I imagine you would prefer to leave before daybreak."

"Cuc, you'll be taking your life in your hands if you do this. It might cost you more than your life. It might cost pain and suffering," Lyss said, feeling deeply at this offer.

Although worried about this crucial trip, Lyss let his mind wander a bit. He recalled how, as a boy, he had driven a wagon with horses on his grandfather's farm in West Virginia. I helped ease his troubled mind to recall his boyhood.

"I'd planned to drive myself, " he said, "going as far as Di Linh on the Saigon highway. Then I thought I'd dispose of the oxen and the cart at Di Linh. I'll take about two days to get there. If Monsieur Harvey's condition will permit, we'll make the walk to the sea in two more days."

"But, Monsieur," Cuc said, "you must have Vietnamese driving the oxen. When you leave the cart, I'll take it on to Saigon and sell the strawberries. There's much less chance of questions being asked, either now or later."

"It's true, Cuc, and I thank you. Sometime I may be able to repay you. Certainly I can give you some money, but that is small compensation for what you are offering. We'll do it. Have the cart ready at three o'clock in the morning."

That evening he busied himself with making up two backpacks for himself and for Harvey, as well as gathering some trail rations together. They would travel light.

From tomorrow, he had five days to meet the scheduled rendezvous with Sarah, Al and Toni.

It was a little past three in the morning when Duong brought the cart into the backyard. It was loaded with strawberries. Duong had placed a light covering of hay over the boxes of berries to protect them from the heat and the sun.

Lyss and Harvey donned the black pajamas. Lyss cleared a padding of hay away from the back of the cart. Harvey slid into the space Lyss had constructed. Lyss put both backpacks into the space with Harvey, handing him the Browning and a stiletto. He kept the belt knife and another stiletto for himself, as well as a small derringer he had obtained.

"Don't speak unless you're spoken to, Harvey, because you can see mighty little from your cubbyhole. We'll try to stop every two hours, about every five miles, if we can find a secure place for you to get out and stretch."

Lyss smiled, then grimaced.

"At last, we're on our way."

The oxen plodded along at what seemed like a snail's pace to Lyss. About four miles out of town, they found a forested area with some small brush and pulled in there.

Lyss helped Harvey out of the cart. They stood, stretching, in one of the areas fairly well covered by brush.

"It's not so bad," he said to Lyss. "I keep in mind that each roll of the wheels brings me closer to getting out of this goddamned country."

Cuc brought out a loaf of bread and three small pieces of cold meat. They washed it down with water and proclaimed it a good breakfast. Harvey went back into his niche. They headed out on the road again.

The morning light was strong about an hour later when they spotted a roadblock up ahead.

"This is routine under the new regime, Monsieur Juan," Cuc said, speaking French.

"What is your destination," the soldier said. "Let me see your papers."

Cuc explained they were taking strawberries to Ho Chi Minh City and handed over her papers.

One of the soldiers went to the back of the cart and began rummaging in the straw. Lyss laid his hand on his derringer, expecting trouble, but the soldier found one of the big, juicy strawberries, pulled it out, took a bite, then returned to his post.

The first soldier looked at Cuc's papers, handed them back, then held out his hand to Lyss, who handed him his papers.

"If you are Filipino, why are you wearing our national dress?" the soldier asked.

"Because it's comfortable, and I like it."

The soldier handed back the papers and waved Cuc to drive on.

Lyss breathed a sigh of relief.

Near sunset, they came upon another nicely forested area with a grassy glade. They dismounted, again placing Harvey in a bushy area. Cuc and Lyss unhitched the oxen and tethered them on the grass. One at a time, Cuc took the animals to a small brook and let them drink.

Then they prepared a simple supper. Lyss suggested Harvey sleep in his niche in the cart, while Cuc and Lyss wrapped blankets around themselves and stretched out on some soft grass.

The next day was uneventful. Shortly after they had passed through Di Linh, in another forested are, Lyss dismounted and helped Harvey out of his place. Stepping behind some bushes, they put on more conventional clothes, including sturdy GI boots for hiking.

"I was lucky," Lyss said. "I found two pair of American GI boots that would fit us."

They left the Vietnamese dress, including sandals, with Cuc.

Lyss dismantled the bamboo cage, as Harvey had come to call it. They used the wood to make a fire for coffee.

With the cart rearranged, Cuc gave each a strong handshake and moved on down the road with the oxen and the strawberries.

Lyss and Harvey headed east through the woods.

DRAGONS YET TO SLAY

CHAPTER TWENTY-ONE

The *Pharaon* sailed briskly almost due south, tacking into winds that were mostly out of the southeast. On the fourth day they made the shelter of the port of Ranai on the east edge of Netuna Besar in the Kepulauan Islands.

They were welcomed by some acquaintances Al and Toni had made in past visits.

Sarah excused herself and went onshore for a walk. It was nearly an hour later when she returned and joined Al and Toni on the forward deck.

"Al, I'm worried about our situation. Do we have to be four days away from the Vietnam shore? Aren't there any ports closer?"

"Well," Al said, "we're really only three days from our destination, which is downwind from us. As I think I told you, it took us four days to get here, but it will only take three to get back. This is one of the closest and best ports I could reach before the storm that's surely going to hit us by tomorrow."

Blowing wind and heavy rain hit them the next

day. After two days of it the sky cleared.

They enjoyed the respite.

"I've checked with the shortwave on the weather and this blast did not hit Vietnam. It passed west of Vietnam and hit the Malay Peninsula," Al said. "While I'm being such a damned good weather forecaster, Sarah, let me warn you there will be another storm in a few days. It will likely hit the Vietnam coast. I'm afraid it will coincide with our rendezvous. What the hell, we've been lucky so far. If it rains, it will just have to rain, and we will have to ride it out."

"I'm not as concerned about us as I am about Lyss and Harvey, who have two or three days of mountain walking. That's tough enough in good weather, but miserable in a heavy rain," Sarah said.

"If we're at the rendezvous point in a storm, it will make it very difficult to bring them to the boat, won't it?"

"Yes, I'm afraid so," Al said. "But, as you saw on the trip from Manila, the *Pharaon* is a mighty fine seagoing ketch. I suggest we stay here three more days and weigh anchor on the ninth. Maybe the second storm will pass through in the next three days. Except in heavy weather, our return to Hoa Da will be at least a day less than it took us to get here."

"Al," Sarah said, "I know the weather is not your fault. But damn it, this is tough on those two guys ashore. My worry keeps me from being reasonable about it, so forgive me for being a bit curt.

"Can we possibly make the rendezvous point a day or two ahead of schedule? If Lyss can get Harvey there early, I don't expect him to object to one less day in Vietnam."

The second storm hit the island on the eighth and had abated somewhat as it passed on to the north. The *Pharaon* weighed anchor and headed out into rough seas.

For three days they ran before the wind, making good time despite the roughness of the ocean. On the night of the eleventh they arrived off Hoa Da in another rainstorm. Visibility was severely limited. Sarah anxiously stayed with the radio in case a message should come through.

Lyss and Harvey started their walk east through the forest with Harvey in the lead, setting a brisk pace. Lyss was glad to follow along for a change. They moved across a ridge and down a small slope.

"Keep the sun in your face, Harvey," Lyss said. "We need to move slightly south of east and stay along the ridges as much as possible. We have about thirty miles to do. Two days after today will do it easily. Quit trying to set up a racing pace."

All went well for about an hour, when Harvey suddenly halted and grabbed the calf of his right leg.

"Damned muscle cramping."

They stopped and Lyss began to massage the muscle. At last it relaxed.

"You're trying to do too much, too fast, Harvey. You've been cooped up too long, so let's take it easy for a while and get ourselves accustomed to freedom and the mountain air.

"Take a look at the sky to the south. It's the monsoon season. I think we have a big storm coming up. Let's keep our eyes open for a cave or at least a shelter of some kind for tonight."

Harvey remained quiet, but slowed his pace down. They continued to head east. In about an hour, Lyss spotted what appeared to be a cliff overhang in the valley below them, so they went down and looked the place over.

It was near a small stream with the cliff facing north, so Lyss announced they would camp there for the night.

Lyss brought out a machete and attacked some nearby pine trees, cutting first some small branches replete with pine needles. He laid them in the deepest portion of the cliff overhang to be used as beds. Then he cut larger and longer branches and leaned them at the outside of the overhang to offer some shelter from the rain.

Meanwhile, Harvey had gathered deadwood and started a small fire at one end of the shelter.

"Thank God for Boy Scouts," Harvey said. "It's been years, but it seems to have stayed with both of us."

Lyss cooked a scanty but good meal, and as darkness set in, they wrapped up in blankets and went quickly to sleep.

They were awakened by increasing wind. Then sheets of water hit the valley as the monsoon rain struck in full blast. They were dry in their niche, since the rain came out of the south.

"Well, Harvey, let's rest while we can and hope this storm doesn't last too long," Lyss said and curled back up in his blanket.

Near noon the storm abated, but rain still fell lightly.

"Damn it," Lyss said. "I didn't pack rain gear for us, and I knew it was monsoon season. Sometimes I have to be hit over the head with a two-by-four to get my brains working. We can cut holes in these blankets and poke our heads through, using them as ponchos. They will get wet and heavy, but I think it will keep us from getting soaked."

Lyss found a trail, which they followed down the valley. They made slow progress. By late afternoon, with an occasional shower sending them under trees for slight shelter, Lyss figured they had made another ten miles.

"We should be about ten miles from the ocean. I think the Hoa Da mountain we want is south of us. Let's find another spot to camp and see if the storm will let up by morning. I'm willing to bet the *Pharaon* is anchored about ten miles off Hoa Da right now. Tomorrow morning we will go on down this valley to the coast road and take the road south toward Hoa Da. I traveled that route by bicycle just two weeks ago, so I know where to turn and climb up the mountain to increase the radio range to the *Pharaon*.

"The mountains run right down to the sea in this area, so both the highway and the railroad are in the narrow corridor between the mountains and the ocean."

They found shelter under some large trees. The rain had intensified again, making any contact with the *Pharaon* unlikely at best.

They wrapped themselves in their blankets and rested, then slept under the large trees.

Back in Dalat, Vo Van Son called the chief of police and asked him to come to Son's office.

When he arrived, Son said, "My intuition tells me that that Filipino, Juan Farrar, probably had something to do with the escape of the American spy, Zimmerman. Farrar impresses me as a man of ingenuity and ability.

"I think we should alert several places to look for him and Zimmerman, although they might travel separately. Get out the word to the border guards, the beach guards and the airport security at Tan Son Nhut."

"Tell them to look for a middle-sized Filipino and a large American. If Zimmerman is not out of the country, he probably will have recovered some of his weight. Tell them both are dangerous and probably armed. Tell them Zimmerman is either without papers, or any papers he might have will be forged.

"I think I have been taken by that Filipino pig, so I am going to Phan Rang and get a fast boat in case they cross the beach in that area. Farrar visited that area. I now think it was not to check up on piers. Notify me there if you get word."

The police chief accepted the instructions and said, "Yes, sir. We'll get right on it. I think they should be alert for Zimmerman, but I will follow your orders."

Within a few hours all the security forces were on the alert for the American and the Filipino.

The next day the security forces for the beaches near Phan Rang and Phan Thiet were alerted to look for the escapee and his possible companion.

The foot patrols covered the beaches in teams of three. The team from Phan Rang worked south to Hoa Da where it met with the team from Phan Thiet. Both teams reversed directions to return home.

Meanwhile, Lyss and Harvey had rested for the night. By morning the rain was over. They made their way on down the valley, soon coming on the railroad. A few yards farther they reached the highway.

Lyss examined the road and announced they were about two miles north of the mountain which overlooked Hoa Da.

"Let's stay off the highway and walk along the west side of the railroad. I believe we will be less obvious to chance passersby," Lyss said.

"We can't stand a roadblock or passing police or soldiers demanding documents because your documents are zilch. If we hit such a situation, we may have to take positive action, so keep yourself alert and ready."

Harvey agreed. They walked on, coming to a short tunnel through the side of a mountain. They took the chance and walked through the tunnel.

Harvey had cut a small pole early that morning. As they walked through the tunnel he scraped it along the walls.

Lyss rushed to him.

"You stupid son of a bitch! We're in enemy territory. We need extra noise like we need a hole in the head."

"Yes, sir." Harvey said in a loud voice that echoed through the tunnel.

As they emerged, they were greeted by three soldiers who immediately unslung their AK47s and called Lyss and Harvey to a halt.

Speaking in Vietnamese, Lyss said, "We are on our way to Hoa Da. We took a shortcut through the railroad tunnel."

One soldier, obviously the senior of the group, said, "You are obviously not Vietnamese. Let me see your papers."

Lyss reached into a pocket, brought out the papers, and walked slowly toward the soldier. His left hand was in another pocket, holding the derringer out of sight.

"No," Lyss said. "I am not Vietnamese. I am Filipino, and as my papers will show you, I am in this country by invitation of your government to do construction work."

He kept talking as he walked toward the soldier, who turned to Harvey and said, "Bring me your papers, too. I think you are the two men we have been searching for."

Since Harvey had no papers, Lyss quickly brought his left hand out of his pocket, placed the derringer near the soldier's temple and fired. Harvey pulled out the Browning and shot one of the other soldiers, but the third started spraying bullets with his AK47, going for Lyss first. Harvey's quick shot kicked up dirt in front of the Vietnamese. He turned and ran.

Lyss was on the ground, but got up and said to Harvey, "Let him go, Harvey. Let's pick up two AK47s and get out of here. Head up the slope of that mountain."

He pointed toward the next ridge.

Harvey grabbed one of the guns and headed up the slope. Lyss, who had picked up the other AK47, was moving slowly. Harvey came back to him.

"I caught one in the left leg, Harvey, but it seems to have missed the bone. Let's get out of sight first."

Harvey took the lead and began a zigzag pattern up the slope, trying to pick an easy route for Lyss. Lyss kept lagging behind. Harvey went back to him.

"Put an arm around my shoulder and lean on me. Try to take the weight off your left leg."

They picked their way through the small trees. Twice Lyss stumbled and nearly fell.

At last they reached the crest of the ridge. Lyss collapsed and was unconscious. Harvey removed Lyss's walking shoes, then his trousers and laid Lyss on a blanket.

Harvey found bandages in Lyss's knapsack and bound up the wound. The bullet had passed through the muscles of the leg. It was a cleam wound.

Lyss's eyes fluttered. He opened them.

"Thanks, Harvey. Are we pretty well hidden?"

"Not very well, Lyss, but if you can stand for me to carry you, I'll move us into a small grove not too far away and bed you down. You must take it easy."

"Okay," Lyss said. "Find us a little better hiding spot until dark. Then we can move forward on this mountain and reach the *Pharaon* with my dinky radio. We must warn them that beach security has been alerted to look for us. We must tell them about the firefight. That guy who got away will bring more soldiers on the double, you can bet on that. We are in for more shooting. I hope they don't search this mountain and we can make our rendezvous."

DRAGONS YET TO SLAY

CHAPTER TWENTY-TWO

As soon as Lyss was safely bedded down, Harvey nervously suggested he should seek some water.

"I have to wash the blood out of this trouser leg anyway," he said. "I'll be careful and head off to the left, instead of down where we were. You will be all right here in this heavy cover. Just rest quietly."

Harvey took two canteens and the trousers and headed at an angle down the slope. He found a spring, rinsed out the trousers and filled the canteens with clear, cold water.

When he returned to the campsite, he found Lyss wrapped in the extra blanket and asleep.

To the southeast, heavy storm clouds were coming up fast with the full promise of more wind and rain.

Harvey left Lyss quietly sleeping until nearly dark. The trousers had dried. He dressed Lyss again.

"Are you going to be able to make it, or shall we

delay here?" Harvey said.

"I'll make it, Harvey. I must make it."

They started the walk east on the ridge in the dark. Lyss was pale, moved slowly, but was confident. At last they reached the point of the mountain and could observe the ocean.

Lyss had carefully prepared his message. First they used the flashlight, pointing well out to sea. A brief code was answered from only about a mile offshore. Lyss had expected the *Pharaon* to be out farther, but was delighted to find it in fairly close.

Lyss's message was:

Danger. Lyss wounded in firefight. Two enemy killed. Third escaped.

Expect action on beach. May be lucky, but be alert.

Meet you on beach in thirty minutes.

Acknowledge by flashlight.

The *Pharaon* answered A K.

Al set about getting the boat ready. He placed his hunting rifle in the boat and handed Sarah a Smith and Wesson .38.

"Is this too big for you?"

"I've qualified with it as well as the Browning," she said. "I surely hope I don't have to use it."

"I have another weapon you ought to know about, Sarah," Al said. He moved to the bow and indicated a long waterproof box.

"This contains a powerful hand held rocket launcher, with armor piercing capacity. I have kept it in case one of the pirates who frequent the China Sea attacks us."

The wind increased and the first drops of rain began to pelt the *Pharaon*. The ketch pitched as the waves loomed higher.

From the rolling deck, Sarah got into the inflatable boat with Al, leaving Toni to tend the *Pharaon*. They headed for the beach.

As soon as they got the acknowledgement, Lyss and Harvey carefully and slowly began the descent down the mountain toward the beach.

"Keep alert, Harvey. Let's recall our childhood and play Indians sneaking through the woods."

They made their way, with Harvey occasionally helping Lyss in steep places. The pale Lyss kept a grim look on his face and stayed with Harvey at their slow pace.

They came down to the railroad, looking cautiously over the open terrain. Seeing no one, they moved as swiftly as Lyss could to cross the railroad. Just as they started down the tracks on the other side, a voice called in Vietnamese, "Stop!"

They ran into the lesser brush, which covered the ground between the railroad and the highway. The

Vietnamese let go with a burst from an AK47 which fell short of them.

They were into the brush a few yards when Lyss said, "Wait. Maybe we can stall them off. I'm not interested in any more killing, if we can avoid it."

Lyss moved back under cover of the brush to a view of the railroad. He saw three soldiers coming toward him. He fired a burst from his AK47 into the dirt in front of them. They jumped back, hitting the ground behind the railroad tracks.

The weather turned nasty with wind and rain as Lyss quietly rejoined Harvey. They made their way to the highway and toward the beach. They could see the boat from the *Pharaon* still off the beach about a hundred yards. They remained under what little cover they could find on the edge of the beach, hoping Al could get the boat in quickly.

The Vietnamese soldiers had only been delayed momentarily by Lyss's tactics. They were soon visible crossing the road.

Lyss fired another burst into the ground, but this did not stop them. The soldiers kept running toward the beach and the two men they could now see.

Lyss leveled the AK47, fired at the man in the lead. He pitched forward. One of the other soldiers cut loose with a burst at Lyss. Almost simultaneously there came the crack of a hunting rifle from the beach. The second man dropped to the ground and did not move.

Harvey fired at the third man. He turned and ran. Harvey turned to run to the beach and found Lyss lying on the ground, unconscious.

Harvey was sure Lyss had been hit again, but did not take time for an examination. He threw Lyss over his shoulders in a fireman's carry and headed for the boat.

Waves were lashing the beach. The rain was getting heavier. Harvey waded on out to the pitching boat. Al helped him get Lyss into the boat. Al then assisted Harvey aboard, started the motor and headed as fast as he could out into the rough waves.

Sarah rested Lyss's head on her lap. Harvey began ripping Lyss's shirt off, revealing two bullet holes fairly high up in the left chest. He took the ripped shirt, tore it into strips and bound the chest area as best he could.

"He's alive, all right. He's taken three bullets, but I don't think any of them hit vital parts," Harvey said.

"Let's keep him as steady as we can in these rough waves. Al, get to that boat fast."

They bounced a bit. Al headed straight into the waves. The rain became extremely heavy, blocking their view of the *Pharaon*.

They were nearly to the *Pharaon* and could see it dimly in the stormy night when a large wave came at an angle and pitched the light boat up and over. The motor died immediately. Al scrambled to get to the side. Harvey joined him and they began to try to right the boat.

Sarah and Lyss were thrown into the sea. She kept a strong hold on him. Then she took him in a life-saving grip with her left hand and swam toward the *Pharaon* with her right arm.

Going down into the swells and at the bottom of them, she made good headway, but the approaching waves often threw them back as far as she had gone forward. Her greatest effort was to keep Lyss's head enough above the water to insure his breathing. She succeeded and at last got him to the stern of the *Pharaon*.

The *Pharaon* was anchored headed into the wind, the rain and the rough sea. Toni came to the stern and threw a rope to Sarah. She tied it around Lyss's wounded chest and under his arms. As Toni lifted, Sarah pushed. At last they got him aboard.

Sarah climbed slowly aboard, then collapsed on the deck, soaking wet and exhausted.

Al and Harvey had righted the boat. With the motor not operating, they paddled to the *Pharaon*. They latched it to the side. Al hoisted anchor, started the engine and headed out to sea. The *Pharaon* was pitching and rolling.

Harvey went to the stern where Lyss was lying on the deck. The two women helped him get Lyss below deck and into bed. They undressed him and dried him off. Toni brought bandages and antibiotic powder. They dressed his chest wounds. Both shots had passed through cleanly.

Toni told Sarah to get into some dry clothes while she dressed the leg wound, which was no longer bleeding.

"There's nothing to do now but keep him as comfortable as we can in this rough sea and keep him from falling off the bed," Toni said.

"I'll stay here with him," said Sarah. "Now it's your turn to get into dry clothes."

Despite the pitching and rolling of the ship, Sarah managed to get Lyss under the covers. She tucked in an extra blanket to fasten him tightly in the bed.

It would be better if he was kept immobile for a while.

Harvey stayed with Al in the cockpit as the boat headed about sixty degrees off the direction of the wind.

"Let me take the helm, Al," he said. "When are you going to put up a sail? What sail will you use in this storm?"

"We'll put up a try sail in a few minutes, as soon as I am sure we are in international waters. Take the helm and let me watch you a few minutes."

Harvey did a good job. Al went forward to put up the try sail, then cut the engine. They were quiet but slow in moving on toward the east.

Al relieved Harvey at the helm. Harvey went below to get coffee and some food and to see Lyss. Sarah reported he was breathing regularly and did not seem to have developed a fever. Harvey had tears in his eyes as he turned from the bedroom to go back up on deck. Harvey thought that, although he and Lyss had not been good friends, *by God, he saved my life*.

Back on deck, Harvey noted they had entered into a dense fog. Al was navigating by the compass. They were moving slowly with the try sail giving them little speed.

A few minutes later, Al turned to Harvey.

"Listen. Do you hear it?"

"Sounds like a motor boat to me," Harvey said.

"Yes. Approaching from the west," Al said. "I'm afraid they have sent a gunboat out looking for us. It's too bad that last gook got away."

They continued to move silently through the fog.

In a short time they came out into bright moonlight. A moment later, a Vietnamese gunboat emerged from the fog and turned toward them.

There was a cannon shot across the bow and a hoarse voice with heavy accent said, in English.

"Heave to! Prepare for boarding."

Instead, Al turned on the engine, gave it full throttle and did a quick complete turn back into the fog. As soon as he entered the fog, he turned abruptly south.

"I don't think they'll expect us to go south," Al said.

"Harvey, go below and tell Toni to get out the American ensign and hoist it at the stern."

Shortly Toni came up and hoisted the colors.

Having headed south for about ten minutes, Al turned the *Pharaon* due east again and broke out of the fog into bright moonlight. Al could see another bank of fog to the east and headed for it. The Vietnamese gunboat sighted him and came at full speed.

Al had removed the shield from the cockpit. He and Harvey huddled there as the gunboat approached. Then Al veered the *Pharaon* quickly to the north and the more cumbersome gunboat sped by, but sprayed the *Pharaon* with machine gun bullets, apparently without harm.

Al swung the *Pharaon* back east and entered the new fog bank. This time, he veered north. He could hear the gunboat turning south, expecting the *Pharaon* to do as it had the last time.

It was nearly dawn. The first light of day was evident as they emerged from this last fog bank.

"You get back here," Sarah said from below.

Lyss emerged on deck. He was moving unsteadily. His swarthy face had turned a pale yellow from loss of blood.

"You guys got a fight going up here?" he said with a wry smile. As he said that the gunboat again came into view.

"Al, we have to get that bastard before he gets us," Lyss said. "I'll go forward and get that rocket launcher out of the case and take a position on the port side of the bow. As he gets close, maneuver quickly to pass him on our port side, and I'll let him have it."

Sarah and Toni both came up. Al yelled at them to get below and stay there.

Sarah checked with Lyss.

"Go below, dear. We have a brief fight on our hands. I've used this type of rocket launcher many times."

He smiled.

Sarah and Toni went below.

Al turned the *Pharaon* as though to avoid the oncoming gunboat. As she neared, he turned quickly toward her and passed fifty meters to the right.

Lyss was in position, prone on the bow and took careful aim at the waterline of the gunboat. As it passed, he fired, striking it just forward of midship.

There was a mighty explosion. Then another explosion in the engine room. She began to sink rapidly.

Al noted that the dinghy was launched from the rear and three men got in it.

DRAGONS YET TO SLAY

CHAPTER TWENTY-THREE

Alfred set his course for Manila.

"Take care of Lyss," he said to Harvey.

Harvey put up the rocket launcher, then helped Lyss down below and back to bed where he collapsed.

About an hour later the weather began to clear. Al put up all sails. A nice breeze assisted them in heading for port.

Sarah reported at mid-morning that Lyss's fever had begun. Al said they must get to Manila as quickly as possible, even though it was three or more days away.

Toni came in to check on both Sarah and Lyss and found Sarah gently daubing Lyss's forehead with a wet cold cloth. Toni relieved her for a while and suggested she lie down on Toni's bed in the forward cabin. Sarah had been without sleep for thirty hours.

It was that evening, after everyone had eaten, that Sarah called from the bedroom that Lyss was awake.

Harvey and Toni came in. Lyss smiled up at Harvey.

"Well, Harvey," he said in a barely audible voice, "we made it."

"Be quiet, Lyss," Harvey said. "You have a battle ahead of you. It'll be three days before you see a doctor, maybe four. You have three holes in you, but you have someone taking tender care of you."

Lyss looked at Sarah with love in his eyes and whispered, "Indeed I have."

The next day Lyss's fever mounted. He tossed and raved as Sarah tried to keep him as still.

"Keep that damned bear away from me!" he shouted. "Shoot him again!"

At another time he relived Tet and shouted, "Cam, there's more rifle fire in our yard."

Toni took turns with Sarah. Harvey insisted on taking a turn with Lyss's care.

Shortly after the gunboat was sunk, Sarah had sent a brief message to Manila:

En route. Lyss seriously wounded.

A message came back on the second day.

Highest authority says well done and congratulations. Medical assistance awaits your arrival.

The third day of their voyage brought smoother seas and a favorable wind. The *Pharaon* briskly plowed through the South China Sea. By the late afternoon of the fourth day, they entered the harbor at Manila.

When they arrived at the dock, an ambulance was awaiting them.

Dr. Stravinsky and Nurse Williams came from the ambulance to join them.

"We have arranged hospital facilities," Dr. Tom said. "We have an airplane waiting to take you all home as soon as I think Juan can travel."

Lyss was conscious when they brought him out on a litter and put him in the ambulance. He smiled but did not speak. Nurse Williams and the doctor were in attendance. Sarah entered and accompanied them. A car was waiting for the Bennetts and Harvey.

In the ambulance, the doctor and nurse went to work immediately, taking blood pressure and pulse rate. They quickly rigged up for a blood transfusion.

"We had a devil of a time finding A-positive blood." The doctor smiled. "Juan, why do you have to have A-positive blood?"

Ulysses smiled and spoke in a weak voice.

"Only the best, Doc. Only the best."

They arrived at the hospital. Attendants hurried out to rush him into a private cubicle in the emergency ward. The doctor, nurse and Sarah remained in the cubicle, with Sarah "standing guard" as she put it.

The doctor removed the bandages from the chest, examining the front first, then turned him partly to examine the exit wounds. He found the wounds all closed, with no apparent infection. He medicated the wounds and bound them up again. Then he examined the leg wound with similiar good results.

"Amazing! Really amazing," said the doctor.

"Give him another unit of blood, penicillin shots for two days, and I think we can move him."

"Although there does not appear to be any bone or lung damage, we will x-ray to be positive."

In George Overton's home, well west of the hospital, there had been a joyful meeting between Overton, Josh and Harvey, with Al and Toni looking on.

Harvey related his story, with great praise for Lyss's ingenuity, courage and stamina. They had several rounds of drinks, then a dinner with white fish, preceded by a shrimp cocktail and served with white wine.

"Al, I ain't knockin' your galley on your fine ship," Harvey said, with a wide grin.

"But we had nothin' like this. In fact, it's been a long, long time since I had anything to compare."

George called for a brief meeting in his study.

"There will, of course, be a shooting hearing," he said.

"It has been arranged to be done in the Washington vicinity at some unspecified future date. I do not think you or Lyss have anything to worry about."

"Well," Harvey said grimly, "every shot was necessary for us to be successful. The only question might be Lyss's knifing that son of a bitch guard. Maybe Lyss did not have to do it, but that was the guy that poked the electric cattle prod into my balls.

"Lyss said he let him have it for me. And, well, I approve. Maybe the outfit will not, but I damned sure do."

Al and Toni started to leave for the *Pharaon*. Harvey stopped Al at the door.

"In this damned shootin' hearin'," Harvey said, "we will not mention your rifle shot. I will talk to Lyss. I'm sure he will agree that all the killin' was done by him and me."

Al and Toni left. Josh returned to the safehouse. Harvey was invited to stay the night with the Overtons.

The next day Al and Toni visited Lyss in the hospital. They were happy to find him resting easily and in good spirits.

"Guess it's goodbye time, Ole Buddy," Al said. "Glad we all made it. Glad we accomplished the mission. If you ever want to cruise the Pacific, get in touch."

Toni leaned over and kissed Lyss full on the lips.

They departed.

On the third day after their arrival in Manila, Lyss was taken from the hospital to the airport. Sarah, the doctor and the nurse accompanied him. They were met at the airport by Harvey and Josh.

Customs and immigration formalities were waived.

They were taken directly to the plane, a Boeing 707 from the Special Air Missions fleet.

"Why not Air Force One?" Harvey laughed.

"Well," said Dr. Tom. "This one is on the personal order of the President."

While not as well equipped as the famous Air Force One, this plane was luxurious, with two private cabins. There was a full crew, including galley, so in the fourteen hours it took to reach Andrews Air Force Base, they all ate well.

Lyss was encouraged by the doctor to sit up part of the time. He thoroughly enjoyed every minute of it.

DRAGONS YET TO SLAY

CHAPTER TWENTY-FOUR

Formalities were brief at Andrews. All six were taken by helicopter to Walter Reed Army Medical Center.

Harvey was told he must undergo a thorough medical examination. His complaints fell on deaf ears.

"I should have done it in Manila," Dr. Tom said. "But frankly I was primarily interested in being sure we could bring a live Juan back with us.

"After all, you have not been on a picnic. We certainly must take a closer look at that right hand."

Sarah spoke up.

"If I'm not needed, I'm taking a taxi to my home. I'm going to get cleaned up and into some different clothes. These are all worn out. See you in the morning, if that's all right, doctor."

"Fine. Fine. Come about eleven o'clock."

"Let's share a taxi, Sarah," Joshua said. "I'll let you off and go on to Georgetown. I got a friend what'll put me up."

It was two days later. Lyss had the head of his bed elevated. He was reading The Washington Post. A young man entered the room, looked around and waved to the door.

The President entered.

He went over to the bed and shook Lyss's hand.

"Well done, Colonel McCutcheon, well done."

With a quizical expression on his face, the President spoke again.

"You are Colonel McCutcheon, aren't you? Your disguise is good, indeed."

"Yes, Mr. President, it's me. Many thanks for the kind remarks. Special thanks for sending that nice plane to Manila for us."

"I wanted to be sure we got you back here for the finest medical care.

"Colonel, I understand there must be a shooting hearing. If my information is correct — and it damned well better be—you have killed three men. It is my opinion that they deserved to die. Your actions were in line of duty.

"To make certain that you are not subjected to a trial, or anything more than the Agency's hearing, I have issued a classified pardon. It will surface only if it is needed.

"I must go now. They think I am here to visit Senator Aldershot, so I must go pay my respects to him.

"Again, Colonel, my gratitude and my compliments."

"Thank you, Mr. President. I will be back in West Virginia without this disguise before too long."

The President left.

In a few minutes, Ham Campbell entered.

"I thought you should have the opinion of highest authority, Lyss, before I stuck my head in.

"It's good to have you back, all in one piece more or less."

"Mighty good to see you, Ham." Lyss smiled broadly. "Parts of the trip were were real fun."

"As soon as the doctor gives us the go ahead," Ham said, "we'll move you back to Green Acres and begin restoring Lyss McCutcheon to his normal appearance.

"Also, dammit, we have to have a shooting hearing. I will convene that panel at Green Acres. You will return to your farm sooner that way.

"Don't worry about the hearing. It will go well. Even if it doesn't, the President has issued a pardon, which will not surface unless it becomes essential."

Lyss was kept in Walter Reed for a week. Sarah took him to the familiar grounds of Green Acres. Dr. Tom and Nurse Williams started his shots to remove the pigmentation. The third day minor surgery restored the nose to its former shape.

"That is better, Doc, much better."

Sarah arrived about cocktail time. Charles restrained giggles as he brought in a tray of San Miguel beer.

He was greeted with laughs and then a mock stern lecture from Lyss.

"Saint Chivas Regal, Charles, if we have any saints tonight."

Cocktail time was filled with laughter and gaiety. The dinner was one of Charles' best.

As he savored the roast duck, Lyss thought of how good trail rations had tasted on the mountain roads of Vietnam.

There was more frivolity with after dinner drinks, then everyone started for the bedrooms. Sarah and Lyss entered their suite. He took her in his arms.

"How long has it been, Sarah? Too long, too long."

She reached up and kissed him ardently.

"Lyss, my lover, the battle has been won. I love you."

He embraced her and led her into the bedroom.

The next morning as they were enjoying breakfast, Sarah reminded Lyss that they still had work to do.

"I have drafted the main report," she said. "I want you to read it over to see if I have covered everything important. You can correct my errors.

"I also want biographic data, as much as you can give, on General Tran Quoc Nha, Vo Van Son and Tran Van Thiet. I don't need birthdays and that sort of crap, but your assessment of what makes them tick and their attitudes."

They worked together for a couple of days. Sarah prepared to go back to Washington.

"I am going to see the finance people on this trip. You will be compensated for your car, the 'funeral' and your work. How do you want to be paid?"

"I don't know how much the loot will be," Lyss said, "nor do I care. Suppose you bring it to me in cold cash, then I will return to Washington, buy a car and drive back to the farm."

In two weeks, Lyss noted the coffee color of his skin was being replaced with normal color.

He queried Dr. Tom.

"When do you think Lyss McCutcheon can emerge into the world?"

"From a medical standpoint," the doctor said, "probably in another week."

Two days later in the late morning hours a limousine pulled up in front of the mansion. Four men and a woman got out. Harvey was in the lead, wearing a broad smile and a cast on his right hand. They had reconstructed his right thumb.

Lyss recognized Bryan Austin, the General

Counsel of the C. I. A. The others were strangers to him.

"Colonel McCutcheon," Austin spoke firmly, neither hostile nor friendly, "we are here to discuss your latest activity."

"Yes, Mr. Austin," Lyss said. "I have been expecting several people to go over the incidents. When would you like to start?"

"As soon as possible. Let us go inside and set up a couple of tables."

In the television room, they moved one of the larger tables to the center of the room. They placed three chairs at it. They set a smaller table near the big table and another small table with two chairs facing the big table.

As they finished, Austin said, "Gentlemen, and lady, are we ready to proceed?"

They all nodded "yes". Lyss and Harvey were seated at the lone table facing the three. The secretary took out her notebook. A small tape recorder was placed near the front center of the head table. Note pads were placed at each position, including Lyss's and Harvey's.

"This is a Board of Inquiry, assembled on the orders of the Director, to look into the matter of the use of violence in carrying out an Agency mission.

"Colonel Ulysses McCutcheon, I am Bryan Austin. My companions are Justin Smith, Edward McCarty and Miss Eleanor Avery. Do you have any

DRAGONS YET TO SLAY

cause to challenge any of us before we begin this inquiry?"

"No, Mr. Austin," Lyss replied. "I have great confidence that the Agency has selected fair and impartial people to examine my actions."

"All stand. Colonel McCutcheon and Mr. Zimmerman, please raise your right hands. Do you swear that the testimony you are about to give, including responses to all questions, will be the truth and nothing but the truth, so help you God?"

"I do," chorused Lyss and Harvey.

"In your own words, Colonel McCutcheon, please relate to us your activities in April and May of this year, beginning with your landing on the shores of Vietnam."

Lyss related his story in detail, including the rescue of Harvey through the tunnel and the stabbing of the guard.

"Let us pause here to see if there are any questions regarding this action. Mr. Smith?"

"Thank you, Bryan. Colonel McCutcheon would you explain to us why you felt it necessary to kill the guard, whose immobility was scheduled to last at least thirty minutes?"

"Yes, sir. I felt that an examination of the guard when he returned to consciousness might reveal that he had been stunned by one of our technical devices. Secondly, I felt that his death was necessary to cover the story of the exterior escape.

-269-

"However, I must admit to you all that my main motivation was the treatment he had accorded Harvey Zimmerman. It was a most brutal torturing job. He was the leader. It was then and is now my opinion that he deserved to die. I would have preferred to have had him conscious and knowing that he was to die. That shows you the bitterness I felt."

"Let us assume that his actions had merited your displeasure and even hate. What authority did you think you had to kill him?" Smith continued.

"I considered him my enemy at war, Mr. Smith. As has happened in other wars, I had to kill him to achieve my objective."

"I have no further questions in this phase," Smith said.

"Mr. McCarty."

"I have no questions in this phase. I am satisfied with the explanation as given," McCarty said.

Austin looked at his watch and suggested a lunch break.

When they were all seated comfortably, Charles served a shrimp salad with White Zinfandel wine.

After the lunch, with a brief break for rest rooms, the group seated themselves. Austin resumed the hearing.

"Colonel, please continue with your story."

Lyss then related the events following Harvey's removal from prison and the story of Jose Mendoza as well. Then he launched into the details of the trip to Hoa Da. After he had related the story of the soldiers killed at the tunnel, McCarty interrupted him.

"Colonel," he said, "did you not realize that placing the derringer at his head would result in instant death? Why not fire to disable him?"

"We were in a tight spot. When he asked for Harvey's papers — which did not exist — I knew the three of them must be removed. So I took the initiative with the leader. A wounded man can do a lot of damage with an AK-47, Mr. McCarty."

Neither Smith nor Austin pursued the matter further. Lyss went on with the trip, telling of Harvey taking the lead over the wounded Lyss.

"Perhaps it would be better for the rest of the story to be told by Mr. Zimmerman," Lyss said. "I was unconscious during part of the time."

"First, Mr. Zimmerman, is there anything in what Colonel McCutcheon has said that you challenge or are there any items upon which you would like to elaborate?"

"Only if Lyss had given me the stilleto and a few more minutes, I not only would have killed that son of a bitch in the prison, I would have cut out his balls and stuffed them in his mouth."

"Hardly a civilized point of view, Mr. Zimmerman," Austin said. "But I do not think you were regarding him as a civilized person."

"Correct. Nor were his actions civilized, Mr. Austin."

"Now, Mr. Zimmerman, take up the story with the second group of soldiers near the Hoa Da beach."

Harvey then related the story as he saw it, complete with Lyss's warning shots and attempt to avoid further bloodshed. He did not mention Alfred Bennett.

"Any questions, Mr. Smith?'

"None."

"Any questions, Mr. McCarty?"

"None."

"Then you gentlemen are excused. We will go into executive session to arrive at an opinion."

Harvey and Lyss went out onto the veranda. Lyss noted that it was mid-afternoon. He called on Charles for "a bit of libation". Charles brought him a scotch. Harvey took a bottle of the San Miguel.

"Can you stay over for a visit, Harvey?"

"No," Harvey replied.

"They have warned me that I must return with them to be available as the results of the hearing move up through channels. That ain't far, from General Counsel to the Director. Besides they want to check up on my right hand and thumb."

The three men and the secretary arrived on the veranda in less than an hour.

"We have reached the conclusion, Colonel McCutcheon, that given the circumstances and conditions, you acted in a fitting manner. Perhaps your judgment might be questioned, but not your motives. We will so recommend to the Director."

Harvey grabbed Lyss and hugged him.

"Dammit, Lyss, we've never really been friends," he said. "Sometimes we have competed against each other. Now it is all different. You've saved my life. It's as simple as that. I'm in your debt forever. I want us, from now on, to be friends."

"Sure thing, Harvey."

They embraced. Then Harvey said goodbye.

DRAGONS YET TO SLAY

CHAPTER TWENTY-FIVE

A few days later, Sarah returned with a bulky bank cash bag.

"You pirate," she smiled.

"Your total in this bag is $33,645.50 in cash. The finance department insisted on paying your $14,127.50 compensation by check. There was a 28 percent deduction for good old IRS. All you have to do is sign these two vouchers.

"Here is a West Virginia driver's license, some credit cards and other identification. The new wallet is a gift from yours truly."

After a wonderful night together, they left for Washington the next morning.

En route, Sarah spoke, a bit saucily.

"I have ten days leave. If I am asked, I would be delighted to spend them on your mountain, which, for some strange reason, I have never seen."

"Madam," Lyss said, "it gives me great pleasure to hand you this engraved invitation for two weeks in paradise.

"If I may stay at your place tonight, I will use your phone and let Connie and Bobby Lee know that the old man made it. I understand the story for public consumption is something like this.

"I picked up a hitchhiker just out of Staunton. About twenty miles out, he pulled a gun and took everything out of my pockets. He had me continue driving. As we started down the mountain on the other side, near Germany Valley, the brakes failed and we plunged off the road.

"Apparently, I got out without injury. I don't remember anything until the other day I realized I was in Philadelphia and that I was Lyss McCutcheon. I had no papers because the thief had taken them from me."

Sarah laughed.

"That's the best we could come up with."

When Lyss called Connie that night, it was one of the few times he had heard her cry as an adult.

"Dad! Dad! Thank God!"

"I will be home tomorrow. I'm bringing Sarah Sanford with me. My story is a long one."

He chuckled.

"Most of the story will remain untold."

Then he called his son, Bobby Lee. He was not as emotional as Connie but was equally as delighted.

Lyss and Sarah had a quiet dinner.

That morning, Lyss bought a new Oldsmobile.

As they got into the car, Lyss turned to Sarah.

"Do you mind if we drive down to the Mall before we leave town? I have a friend I want to see."

"You're the driver, lover boy."

So they drove toward town. When they reached Constitution Avenue, Lyss turned west and came to the Lincoln Memorial.

He circled. As he passed the great somber face, he spoke, almost to himself.

"I made it back, Abe."

Then he headed west to Front Royal and turned south onto the Blue Ridge Parkway.

"Doesn't seem too long ago, does it Sarah."

"No, but this way is nicer," she responded.

"Well, we're not in any hurry, so I'd like to drive along the Blue Ridge Parkway for a few miles. You can see the vastness of Virginia and the beauty of the Shenandoah Valley from this gorgeous, scenic route."

They did not talk as they drove along, finally turning into Staunton and west on Route 250. They passed over the first range and started the descent into Germany Valley.

"Familiar, my love?" he said. It was the place where the "accident" had been staged.

"Yes, the beginning of a long adventure. It had its ups and downs, mostly ups, thank God."

They headed on to the west. Soon he was driving up Logan Run to the cemetery and turned back along the ridge. He took the slightly improved road, which he owned.

Coming around the second mountain, about 400 yards away was the glistening white farm home.

Tears came to Lyss's eyes as he realized how close he had come to never seeing this place again.

"How beautiful!" Sarah exclaimed.

In a few minutes they were parked. Connie came dashing out of the house. She hugged her father, almost unwilling to let him go.

Then she turned to Sarah Sanford.

"Sarah, I am Connie. Welcome to Mount Olympus Farm."

The next few days were wonderful for Lyss. He walked in the woods and on the trails with Sarah. He showed her this scenic place that he had made more livable by fixing up the house and more beautiful by regrading the road, cutting brush from under the trees, trimming the grass here and there. All these were chores of love where he had spent three happy years.

The two weeks slipped by, all too fast.

In the evening they were sitting on the porch sipping drinks and watching the fading light on Cheat Mountain.

"Here I was when it all started," Lyss said. "A phone call from Ham.

"I hope this is where I am when it all ends.

"Sarah, my love, will you share it with me?"

Sarah turned to look at him. A tear started down her cheek. Then she spoke.

"For some time now, I have known that you were going to ask me. I love you very much. I know you love me.

"But there are complications. I cannot see the answer right now. Perhaps we can reach a mutual accommodation.

"I have been on my own these many years. Six or eight more years of service will qualify me for retirement on my own. The timing depends on the powers that be at that time. I would like to finish my service. That will certainly call for one or two more tours overseas.

"I have observed several of the cases where the husband has retired and accompanies his wife overseas as her 'dependent'. Some have worked. Some have not.

"I find it hard to visualize you as a house husband. You are, by nature, a dominant person. That is one of your characteristics which I admire.

"So, I cannot share this lovely place with you now. The time may come. I pray that it does.

"I have mountains yet to climb, dragons yet to slay."

There was a long pause.

Lyss had listened attentively. He swirled his drink in the glass, pondering the problem.

"Success in a marriage depends on many things.

"First of all, of course, is love. We have that. Then there is the mutuality of life together. It is hard for the dominant male to subjugate himself, just as it is hard for a strong willed woman to give up some of her prerogatives.

"Like Chinese bamboo, we must each bend with the wind.

"If you are willing to postpone our life here for the years it will take to qualify you for retirement, then I am willing to set it aside and accompany you anywhere in the world.

"Let me share the future years with you.

"I believe it will sweeten our lives to know that we have this lovely place to come home to some day.

"Meanwhile, let me go with you on your dragon hunt."

Smiling broadly, Lyss took her in his arms. She lifted her lips to his.

"I'm sure," Lyss said, "I can find an interest of my own wherever you are assigned. One of the most successful marriages I know was Diane and Julius

Burton. He went overseas with her and spent a lot of time running embassy PXs.

"Can I get us a preacher, darling? When and where?"

"Here on our mountain," Sarah replied, "and soon, my lover, soon!"

DRAGONS YET TO SLAY

EPILOGUE

Cool morning breezes wafted across the fairways of Brookhollow Country Club in Dallas on a day in late June. Jim Shaw leaned on his driver, watching others of the foursome try to match his 250-yard drive. He recalled Leilehua Golf Course in Hawaii, where Jim and Lyss had enjoyed many an afternoon.

Jim wondered if Lyss had succeeded. He realized he would only know when he heard from Lyss, a Christmas card or perhaps a phone call. If he heard from him, it would mean he was alive. If he was alive, he would have succeeded.

Jim recalled a class he had had in CIA in his early days, dealing with compartmentation. There was a rigid rule in the intelligence business. Each participant in a project was given only what he needed to know and no more. A person might make a major contribution to one part of the project, but never know the final story.

Lyss and Sarah were high above the Atlantic in a Boeing 747, watching the movie and holding hands.

They had taken off from Dulles Airport that morning. Their destination was Sarah's new assignment to Vienna.

Across the Potomac in a huge building at Langley, Harvey Zimmerman flexed his right hand and felt no pain.

Miles further north in Maine, Joshua Rosenbloom was discussing the weather with a ham operator in Spokane, Washington. Maine was enjoying beautiful spring weather. It was already summer in Spokane.

On a cool beach of a remote island in the South Pacific, Alfred and Antoinette Bennett lay happily in each other's arms.

In Dalat, in a thoughtful mood at supper, Vo Van Son wondered how that Filipino pig had done it.

ABOUT THE AUTHOR

Colonel Vincent M. Lockhart of El Paso served 20 years with the Central Intelligence Agency. For two years he was Assistant to the Director, then Allen Dulles, and for four years he was an Inspector on the staff of the Inspector General when John McCone was Director. He retired in 1972 after four years in Vietnam.

He is also retired from the U.S. Army Reserve, with 15 battle stars on his service ribbons.

His decorations include the Legion of Merit and the Bronze Star from the Army, the Intelligence Medal of Merit, the Certificate of Distinction and the Certificate of Exceptional Service from the CIA, the Pershing Medal and the Patrick Henry Silver Award from the Military Order of the World Wars.

Colonel Lockhart is the author of a published book of military history — "T-Patch to Victory" — about the 36th ("Texas") Division in the final ten months of World War II.

He has held several offices of responsibility in The Military Order of the World Wars, a patriotic organization of officers who have served on active duty with the U.S. Armed Forces.

He was graduated from the University of Missouri in 1936 with a degree of Bachelor of Journalism and served as reporter, editor and publisher in the newspaper business before entering CIA in 1952.

Colonel Lockhart and his wife of more than half a century have lived in El Paso, Texas, since1977.